Calliope and the Sea Serpent

Alex McGilvery

I0587628

Calliope and the Sea Serpent

Alex McGilvery

Cover Design by A.P. Fuchs
Interior Illustration by Abigail Horn

For information contact:
http://alexmcgilvery.com

ISBN 978-1-7751286-0-1

Celticfrog Publishing

Chapter 1 The Call to Adventure

Calliope followed Sir Shillingsworth through a vast collection of grotesqueries – creatures suspended in huge bottles filled with murky liquid, others stuffed and set in tableaux. Sculptures of horrific death, paintings of deformed people.

Her father took no notice of what surrounded him; tall, with his grey hair cut severely and great coat flapping like a cloak in the wind, he swept past giant skeletons, not even glancing aside. Calliope itched to get lost in the collection, sketching what she saw. That skill was the reason he employed her. Why he'd ordered her to attend this meeting was beyond her. She had specimens to draw and catalog from the expedition he'd returned from a couple of months ago.

Unless he thought some feminine distraction would aid in his negotiations. Calliope brushed at her dress, covered with pockets she'd added and

1

spotted with charcoal and graphite. In that case, he should have brought someone worth looking at.

Pentam, Sir Shillingsworth's protégé, rolled his eyes and shook his head. He had dressed immaculately in the latest fashion, dark hair perfectly arranged, and took his position as high society scientist very seriously. She caught occasional flashes of humour in those blue eyes. Calliope took a deep breath; she could put up with the boy for the short time she was forced into his presence.

They arrived at the end of the hall, where Sir Shillingsworth looked at Cal as if he had just met her there.

"Really, Calliope, you should take more care with your appearance."

She made a deliberately sickly attempt to show feminine wiles.

"You should have warned me I was to send lust through Lord Carroway's veins."

Pentam's snort echoed through the hall.

"Fat lot of good that would have done." He immediately paled and held his hand up defensively. "I don't mean that in a disparaging way to you, Cal." But he was looking at Sir Shillingsworth as he spoke.

"You should stick to your convictions." A pang struck through her heart before she ruthlessly quashed it. "Nevertheless, you aren't the only one whose words occasionally come out a little sideways of their intent." He spoke nothing but the truth. From her blackened fingers to indeterminate brown hair stuffed in a bun to keep it out of her eyes, even in the finest of gowns, she'd never make any male catch his breath.

"What I meant is, rumour has it Lord Carroway is not, er... set aflame by feminine beauty."

"Then it is a good thing you take all too much care with *your* appearance." Sir Shillingsworth rapped on the door as Pentam turned a series of lovely shades of red. Cal smiled sympathetically at the boy. Her father had little time for niceties, and none for anything less than the bald truth. "Dressing well isn't always about seduction." Sir Shillingsworth eyed Cal again. "Sometimes it is about respect."

The door creaked open as Pentam fought for composure.

How appropriate. Have they treated the hinges to produce the sound? Cal knew better than to give them more than the slightest glance as they paraded into the room. But her mind listed ways she might have created that wonderful groan.

Lord Carroway stood by the window in what had to be a conscious pose, as the fog meant he gazed heroically into nothingness. He looked to be hardly taller than Cal, but at least twice her weight. Expensive tailoring made him look rich rather than gluttonous.

3

"Yes, thank you, James. That will be all. Maybe refreshments at a suitable interval?"

The man who'd let them in closed the door with another delicious creak, then vanished through a side exit which didn't so much as whisper.

Cal hid her delight behind a polite smile as Lord Carroway's eyes passed over her and landed on Pentam. The man almost licked his lips.

"This expedition you wish to send me on?" Sir Shillingsworth stepped forward and claimed the centre of attention. Cal pulled a sketchbook from her pocket along with a stick of charcoal. Her fingers recreated the scene before her – the Lord barely containing his lust, the boy valiantly not fleeing the room, Sir Shillingsworth looking at Lord Carroway like a hawk at a mouse.

"Oh yes, yes. Please be seated." The Lord sat with practiced grace then bobbed up to his feet when his guests remained standing.

"Time is valuable, my Lord. I'd prefer to deal with the business at hand."

"Very well." Lord Carroway pouted and walked to his desk.

Cal's fingers danced across the page. He was perfect, looking longingly at his chair, then picking up a map to hand to Sir Shillingsworth. His fancy clothes and lace contrasted with the practical but high quality suit her father wore.

"I want you to take an expedition to the Sargasso Sea and capture a sea monster for my collection."

Pentam barely contained another snort. Cal let a smile flit across her face. Sir Shillingsworth unrolled the map, glanced at it briefly, then passed it to Cal. She put her sketchbook back in its pocket and pulled folded paper from a different pocket along with a graphite pencil.

"May I?" Cal put map and paper on the desk and nodded at the chair. Lord Carroway jumped, as he might if his settee had spoken to him. He fluttered his hand which Cal took as permission. She sat to copy the map.

"Yes then, where was I?"

"Sea monster." Sir Shillingsworth's voice was a study in neutrality.

"I've heard stories that sea monsters inhabit the Sargasso Sea. You will bring me one."

Cal's lips twitched as she imagined the exact expression on her father's face.

"They are a myth, quite difficult to capture."

"It is my money." Lord Carroway made no effort to hide his petulant tone. "After all the trips I've sponsored, I think I deserve to set the goal for one."

"The Sargasso Sea is understudied, Sir, and might be worth the trip on its own account."

Pentam, getting revenge for being used only for his appearance? If it bothered him so much, why did he constantly fuss over it?

"Very well." Sir Shillingsworth sent a glare at Pentam which ought to have left him but smouldering ash in its wake. "I will assemble a company and find a suitable steamship. I do not intend to waste time waiting for a feckless breeze."

"I would expect nothing less." Lord Carroway wandered behind Cal and peered over her shoulder. "Astonishing."

"Her skill is why I employ her."

"Indeed, perhaps I may glance at the sketchbook she was holding earlier."

More observant than I thought.

"That sketchbook is to Calliope, what a diary is to a Lady." Sir Shillingsworth frowned at the Lord. "Would you expect to peruse the pages of such a book?"

"No, of course not, it's just..." Lord Carroway trailed off. Cal lifted her head and raised an eyebrow ever so slightly. Sir Shillingsworth's nod was just as scant.

"With your permission." Cal pulled a roll of paper from yet another pocket. "I could do a quick sketch for you."

The look of delight on the Lord's face was more than worth the price of the expensive paper. She drew him carefully, without her customary speed. The time spent added worth to the portrait.

It also gave her time to make sure the portrait flattered the man.

James returned with a cart, pouring tea for Sir Shillingsworth and Pentam. Cal's mouth watered at the tray of sweets. *Oh well.*

When she'd completed the portrait, Cal took a small bottle from a pocket. She uncorked it and attached a mechanism with a bulb on one end and a nozzle at the other. A squeeze of the bulb sent mist over the paper. After coating the entire paper, she disassembled the contraption, returning it to her pocket. With utmost care, she lifted the paper by its edges and moved it across the desk. Then she brought out an oilcloth, unrolled it and used the rag within to wipe down the desktop. The sharp scent of pine invaded the room as she replaced the rag.

"Quite extraordinary." Lord Carroway stood with his hands behind his back peering at himself looking up from the paper.

"Please don't touch the paper until tomorrow, my Lord. By then the varnish protecting it will have dried."

"I paid hundreds of pounds for a portrait which barely looked human, never mind like me. And this..." He waved his hand. "James, come and look."

The man came over with a cup of tea and plate of sweets which he placed in front of her. He gave her a slight nod and a smile.

"She has captured your essence, my Lord."

"Sir Shillingsworth, have your artist list what materials she needs to record your expedition and I will see she gets them." The Lord's eyes returned to the drawing as surely as a compass pointed north.

"I wasn't planning on her travelling with us."

"Nonsense, I will want to see the journey through her art."

Sir Shillingsworth paused an instant to look at Cal. She tried to keep her nod dignified and not run over to beg him to say yes.

"Of course, my Lord. I will send you her list." Her father gave Cal the tiniest bend of his lips and actually waited for her to finish her tea before sweeping out of the room, pulling Cal and Pentam in his wake.

"That was well done, dear." Sir Shillingsworth helped Cal into the coach as steam puffed from a valve.

"Thank you, Father. I am delighted to finally be able to travel with you."

His lips pursed, but he didn't say anything. Pentam climbed into the front of the machine and set it in gear. They trundled off to her home where they'd put the expedition together.

Cal made a list in her sketchbook of what she wanted to bring.

Chapter 2   Early Steps

The steam carriage pulled up in front of the city house where Sir Shillingsworth stayed on the rare occasions he wasn't out on a scientific expedition.

"Hans, the pressure isn't holding steady." Pentam jumped out from his seat.

"Must be a stuck valve. I will investigate." Hans opened the door and helped Cal out of the carriage, then stood out of the way while her father climbed out.

"Thank you, Hans. We will be heading out again soon, please notify our usual suppliers. Once you have done that, you may work on the carriage."

Whatever else I could say about Father, he treats everyone the same.

"Very good, Sir. Miss DeBantiche has not yet left on her trip to the Baths. Shall I call her back?"

"There will be no need for that. She has earned her time away."

I'm not that hard to live with, am I?

Cal followed Sir Shillingsworth and Pentam into the house. They hung their coats in the closet. Sir Shillingsworth didn't believe in maintaining a large staff. Hans for the outside, his wife as cook and cleaner, and Miss DeBantiche as chaperone for Cal when he travelled.

"Cal, it is imperative the specimens from my last expedition are recorded before we leave."

"Yes, Father." Cal headed to the drawing room where the light was best and the specimens were laid out. "I'm more than half-way complete."

"Do not rush."

"I will take the same amount of care I always do." Cal couldn't keep the edge from her voice. She knew her work was essential to the scientific value of her father's expeditions. No shoddy drawing would risk his reputation.

Her father nodded at her, then dragged Pentam into the study.

The drawing room, a lovely ironic name given what Cal used it for, flooded with light from the north windows. Tables filled the room. Animal skins and skeletons covered them. Plants and flowers were pressed in heavy journals. Insects floated, pinned to boards. Cal picked up the large sketching board and moved to where she'd left off when her father had called her that morning.

"Miss Calliope." Hans knocked on the door.

"Hans, please call me Cal."

"Your father would have my head."

"How may I help you?" Hans was determined to preserve a dignity Cal didn't care about, but she wouldn't bother him with argument.

"Do you have time to draw some parts for me?"

"Certainly." Cal lay down her pad and pencil.

Out in what used to be the stable, the steam carriage sat, parts laid in exact order on a table. On the wall, Hans had pinned a schematic Cal drew for him back when they bought the machine. She'd copied it from the original on the wall of the man who built the carriage.

"Here." Hans pointed to a part still attached to the carriage. "This is the leak. It's supposed to control the amount of steam driving the gears. On a locomotive, it would be massive and properly sealed. This is too thin and the steam is finding even the slightest flaw in the metal. I need you to draw it in place and to scale so I can show the machinist what I need, and what space I have to work with.

Hans had been with them as long as Cal could remember, his stocky frame apparently ageless. He'd secretly let her help with the horses, and now with the steam carriage.

"Certainly." Cal picked up the sketchbook she kept in the stable for this purpose and took a pencil from her pocket. In a few minutes, she'd sketched the part from several angles and added a scale to the drawings. "What does the inside look like?"

"The inside? I'm not sure. This lever is attached to some kind of plate which opens and closes to control steam pressure and flow. I suppose it's a flat circle just enough smaller than the pipe to turn."

Cal pushed the lever back and forth. She closed her eyes to envision the mechanism. A plate wouldn't be strong enough against the pressure. She'd make a ball, with a hole one way through the middle. It could pivot and close off the valve securely. No leaks.

"There's something which stops it from going too far. Makes sense, the driver wouldn't be able to exactly line up the plate to seal the pipe." She drew what she imagined inside. "Ask him if he could build something like this instead of using a flat plate. It won't leak nearly as much. The extra cost will be balanced by having it more reliable. If this works as well as I imagine, get him to make each valve this way."

"I'll ask." Hans ran his finger across the sketch. "I have no idea how you come up with these things, but you've never steered me wrong yet."

"I get pictures in my mind about how it should work, and how it could break. I can't explain it. I'm just glad to help."

"Thanks, Miss Calliope."

***

Pentam breathed slowly through his nose. As important to his ambitions as Sir Shillingsworth was, he could also be extraordinarily irritating.

"Since this expedition is your notion, you may start the planning of what we will need to accomplish our goal. I will be most interested in how you plan to capture this sea serpent of Lord Calloway's." In private, Sir Shillingsworth's voice dripped with scorn. "I will inform the Society that my next trip to the Cathayn Mountains will be delayed. Given the season, probably by a year."

"I will have a preliminary plan for you by the end of the week." Pentam dropped into the chair at his desk in the corner and pulled his journal toward him.

"I am more interested in quality than speed." Sir Shillingsworth frowned. "A plan is no help if I must redo it."

Pentam clenched his fist, but bit his tongue.

Sir Shillingsworth left the room and Pentam relaxed. He rolled his head to ease the ache in his shoulders. If he wanted to be the famous scientist of his dreams, he needed to keep his position. University graduates in the sciences were churned out in droves, but only Pentam had been chosen to be Sir Shillingsworth's assistant. His previous assistant had a position as curator at a prestigious museum.

He got up and walked over behind Sir Shillingsworth's desk and ran his fingers across the journals lined up on the shelf. The last sea voyage was before Pentam's time, but the man never threw anything away. *There.*

Pentam pulled out the book and carried it over to his desk. A simple copy wouldn't be enough, but the list from ten years ago would be a good starting place. He opened the book and lost himself in the plans.

***

Supper was a roast chicken, cooked all day to make it tender. Pentam ate with a good appetite. Food on the expeditions was never this good. This would be his third excursion, and he looked forward to the novelty of a sea voyage. At least he wouldn't be at risk of freezing to death in the Sargasso Sea.

Cal ate slowly, tasting a bit of everything, occasionally nodding to herself, perhaps cataloging the meal as she did the specimens they brought home. He had to admit her talent was extraordinary. As a science student, he'd been expected to be able to draw adequately to record his findings, but he couldn't imagine having either the speed or accuracy of Cal's work.

If she was coming on this voyage, Sir Shillingsworth would be distracted by her presence. Pentam didn't know what it meant to his position, but his stomach curdled. He'd worked hard to learn everything he needed to impress his employer enough to be counted as a full member of the team. Now she would be joining them simply because she was good with a pencil.

In the morning, Pentam headed out to talk to the people in the merchant houses who oversaw the shipping of goods past the region they would be studying. The newest information about their goal was essential.

It turned out the people with the information he needed were all at sea. He left requests for the captains to contact him upon return to port. As he wandered out of the third merchant office, he was waved to the side by a clerk.

"Sorry, but you must wait until they have finished posing for the photograph."

"Photograph?" Pentam's heart speeded up. He'd seen photographs displayed in some of the wealthy homes of those who sponsored the voyages. If he could learn to take pictures like those, he'd have a way to hold his own against Cal.

When the clerk finally let Pentam enter the foyer of the building, the photographer was still packing up his gear.

"Excuse me, Sir." Pentam stopped a careful distance from the equipment. "I am interested in learning about photography."

"You don't look wealthy enough to afford the hobby." The man didn't look up from his packing.

His brown hair could have used a trim, but his hands were clean and dexterous.

"I am thinking of using it to record a scientific expedition."

"Interesting." The man handed Pentam a crate, heavier than he'd expected but not unmanageable. "Come with me then."

Pentam followed the man out to a horse-drawn buggy. The photographer packed away the gear like it was fine crystal. He climbed up onto the driver's bench.

"Well, are you coming, lad? Name's Alistair McNaught."

"Pentam Booksdale."

They drove slowly, staying out of the way of faster vehicles. Alistair shook his head at the steam carriages as they passed, making the horse shuffle to the side.

"What do they do if it breaks down?"

"Happens a lot." Pentam pointed to where one had pulled over with two men poking around the boiler. "They have a long way to go before they're as reliable as a locomotive. It's trying to make the engine so small. The parts are more delicate. It doesn't help that most people have no conception of how they work."

"And you do?"

"I can explain the physics behind the engine, but I'd be as helpless as the next man if I was asked to repair one. We are fortunate to have a man who is very good with the machines."

"So you take those contraptions on your expeditions?"

"Not normally, but our next one is a sea voyage, and we'll be on a steamship."

"Heh." Alistair guided the horse through an open gate into a tiny courtyard. They unhitched the horse and pushed the buggy into the stable.

Pentam burned with impatience to learn more about the photography, but Alistair rubbed down the horse, gave it fresh water and hay before he turned to unpacking the gear from the buggy. Once again Pentam carried the oddly heavy crate and followed Alistair into the house.

Alistair put his gear down in a side room, then waved Pentam on to a door at the end of the hall. He opened it and revealed a room with all sources of light removed.

"The camera takes the photograph, but this is where the magic happens." He grinned at Pentam. "Don't worry, I know it's chemistry. You could probably explain it all to me, but when you see it, you'll agree it looks like magic."

The first part of the process took part in absolute darkness.

"You got to set up your room where you can lay your hands on what you need with no mistake. Put the wrong solution in at the wrong time and you've wasted your time."

After a light splashing of water, Alistair tugged at Pentam's arm.

"Come, we're done here for the day. Negative's got to dry. I'll show you the camera now."

Back in that side room, Alistair set up three legs with a platform on the top, then put a box on top. He fastened the box and stand together then put a large black cloth on the box. Pointing to a cover on the front, he took it off, then helped Pentam under the cloth.

"Look through the wee hole there."

"Everything's upside down!" Pentam stared, fascinated, through the camera.

"Aye. There's no film in there now. This is where we put the film in." He showed Pentam a slot at the back of the box. "Once you put the film in, you can't see through the camera, so make sure it's pointed right." He handed Pentam the cover from the front of the camera. "Put this on before you load the film. The plates are glass, but the important part is the coating. It's got silver in it which turns black."

Pentam nodded, recalling something from a lecture about the chemistry of photography. He'd review his notes later.

"This is important." Alistair took the cover back and put it over the lens. "You need lots of light to get a good picture. Uncover the lens and count to thirty, maybe longer if the light's bad."

"That won't work well on a ship." Pentam's disappointment wrenched at his gut.

"Some use flash powder to add light, but I don't expect that'd go over well either."

"I'll have to think about it, maybe there's another way to create enough light."

"You figure it out, son, every photographer will thank you."

"Right. So the image is on the glass. What were you doing in that room?"

Alistair pulled a glass sheet from a slot in his desk. "The silver needs help to make the image strong enough to see. That gives you this. It's backward, a negative we call it. The more light, the darker the silver. Once it's dry we'll use it to expose a paper covered with silver to light and get this." He handed Pentam a paper. He compared the image to the one on the glass.

"Amazing." He looked around the room. "You talked about needing to be rich to afford the hobby."

"Aye, t'ain't cheap, but happens I have some spare equipment you can use. I wouldn't mind being a patron of the sciences, considering the sciences have given me my living."

Pentam opened his mouth, but couldn't think of anything to say.

"You come by tomorrow and I'll start training you. Could use a hand with the gear, and the best way to learn is by doing."

Chapter 3 A Gathering Team

The door shuddered under someone's hammering. Cal muttered under her breath as she wiped oil from her hands and walked toward the door. She and Hans had almost finished testing the new valves.

Sir Shillingsworth forbade running in the house for anything less than an ongoing disaster. Obeying his rules to the letter had been one way Cal kept him close while he traveled the world.

She reached the door and opened it. A frowning man in wrinkled travel clothes stood on the step, trunk set on the cobbles behind him. Brown eyes sized her up and dismissed her.

"I apologize for making you—"

"Shillingsworth needs to hire a higher class of servant. If you were that slow to answer the door in my household, you'd be sacked." A man barely taller than Cal brushed past her and looked around the hall. "Given his reputation, I would have thought he'd do better for himself."

Cal bit her tongue and considered her options. She didn't want to embarrass one of her father's colleagues, but this man's attitude made her want to scream. *Politeness, I can always be rude later.*

"Again, my apologies," Cal said. The man turned and glared at her, opening his mouth to speak. Cal beat him to the punch. "My father asked me to greet you, Dr. Gostan. I will show you to the parlour where you can relax. Have your man leave your luggage with Hans and he'll take it up to your room."

Dr. Gostan's mouth flopped like a gasping fish as he turned white, then purple, then green. Cal watched with professional interest.

"This way." She headed down the hall. The unsteady clop of his feet followed her. The parlour had been opened, aired out, and topped up with what Pentam had determined necessary to keep scientists happy while final preparations were made.

Once Dr. Gostan, still apparently bereft of speech, had been installed in the parlour, Cal went to her room to change. She hung the oil-spattered smock on a hook she'd asked Hans to install which would hold it clear of anything it could soil. A rag soaked in turpentine cleaned any errant grease off her hands.

Cal looked in the mirror.

Nope, still no beauty, but no grease in my hair. Or at least not that much. She used the rag to remove it. That done, a quick brush and she twisted her hair into a comfortable bun.

A dress from the little-used side of the wardrobe might placate the poor oaf downstairs. She chose one with subtle colours, then headed downstairs. Caught between finishing her work on the last expedition, and the wait for this one to begin, Cal had been appointed to welcome the guests as they arrived.

As she reached the bottom of the stairs another knock directed her steps toward the door.

"Good day, you would be Dr. Franklyn? Father is out, and asked me to make you welcome."

"Thank you, my dear. The locket Shillingsworth carries doesn't do you justice." Dr. Franklyn took her hand briefly. "I left my luggage with Hans. Is that right?"

"Yes." Cal stepped back and took the doctor's coat to hang in the closet. "If you'd follow me to the parlour."

Dr. Franklyn dressed in brown tweed pants and a shirt with no collar. When he'd removed his flat cap, it revealed a bald spot making him look like a religious brother. His eyes twinkled at her, and Cal had the feeling they would have for a maid too.

By the time her father came home, four scientists were gathered in the parlour, and from the level of sound, were engaged in spirited debate.

"Who's here?" Sir Shillingsworth asked as he hung his coat up.

"Dr. Gostan arrived early, and caught me before I had a chance to change. Dr. Franklyn arrived within the half hour, followed by Prof. Ordin and then a man who insisted I call him Lahdin. They are in the parlour."

"Very good, do you plan to join us?" Sir Shillingsworth walked down the hall to the parlour.

"I am a member of the expedition," Cal said, "but not one of the scientists. I don't want to get in the way of any scientific discussion."

Her father turned into his study and sat behind his desk.

"Are you sure you want to do this?" He steepled his fingers and looked steadily at her.

"Go along on this expedition and be part of discovering new things?" Cal's gut twisted. Her father had been growing less enthusiastic about her being part of the team. He hadn't said as much, but she'd gradually been excluded from meetings with sponsors of the trip. "Of course I want to go. Lord Carroway expects me to be on that ship and making a journal of whatever we encounter. "

"Some would say a ship, even a science vessel, is no place for a young lady." Sir Shillingsworth leaned forward, his face turning red.

Cal knew no other person he allowed himself to show any emotion to; not even her mother, not even at her funeral.

No mercy.

"Good thing Miss DeBantiche has never been able to mold me into a lady." Cal glared at him. "It has been a frequent complaint. I'm twenty-one, and I think you must accept by this time, me being a lady is highly unlikely."

Her father's mouth opened and closed several times during her tirade. His colour so high, she feared he might fall dead of apoplexy. Instead he slumped down into his seat and sighed deeply.

"That has been more my failure than yours, perhaps if I'd been around more—"

"While I cherish your company, Father, my argument with being a lady is that it is stultifyingly dull. They do needlework, pour tea, gossip about eligible bachelors. I have no interest in any of that. My talent can serve science, serve you."

"You may have mistaken my intent, Calliope. I have heard from several people who are normally enthusiastic sponsors that they are concerned about a young woman taking part in a dangerous venture. If you come, you will butt up against that attitude yourself. Are you prepared to deal with it?"

"At least I didn't stab that Dr. Gostan with my palette knife," Cal blurted out, still processing the notion that her presence might threaten the expedition. "If you'll be short of money because of me—"

Her father held up his hand. "I am a man of my word, and Lord Carroway has a great deal of influence. No matter their reservations, our sponsors do not wish to anger him."

"I do want to come, and more, be useful." Cal snapped her mouth shut before she started babbling.

"Very well, Calliope. You will come as our artist and recorder. I will show you how I'd like you to keep the log. While we are on this expedition you will call me Sir Shillingsworth; too much familiarity may breed discontent among the others."

"Only if you call me Cal. I have no idea what possessed you and mother to name me after a circus organ."

"Calliope was the Greek muse of poetry...very well, Cal. Welcome to the expedition. You will be paid twenty pence a day, but will be expected to contribute out of that amount for general supplies and food. Lord Carroway has purchased what you require for your art." Sir Shillingsworth opened a drawer and slid a paper across the desk to her. "Here is the standard contract, please read it and sign it. You may return it to me tomorrow." He opened a new ledger and made a note. Cal couldn't suppress the grin on her face, but she did keep from dancing around the room in excitement. She took the paper, rolled it, and slid it into her sleeve.

"Cal," her father said so softly she almost didn't hear him, "there will be a time when you regret your decision." She started to protest, but he held up his hand again. "There *will* be a time, as there was for me when I wasn't much older than you. When it arrives, do not let it fill you with doubt. Stay the course." He looked up at her. "Please join the others in the parlour, I will be along shortly."

Cal slipped out the door before dancing in the hallway.

"Whatever are you doing?" Pentam set a box, tripod and a bag bulging with other gear on the floor with great care.

"Sir Shillingsworth has hired me to go on the expedition."

"I thought that had been decided by Lord Carroway."

"Father, being a father, needed to be convinced. I'm not just tagging along. I have a contract to sign and must pay to help buy things."

"Congratulations, I guess." He waved at the gear on the floor. "Would you mind helping me carry this to my rooms?"

"Sure, what is it?"

"A camera." Pentam handed her the tripod and picked up the box and the bag. "I wanted to be able to record the expedition, we won't always have a talented artist with us. I met a photographer who liked the idea of being a sponsor of our expedition."

"How fascinating, you must show me how it works."

Pentam gave her an odd look before taking the tripod and disappearing into his room.

Cal hurried downstairs and over to the parlour.

Beth, Hans' wife, stopped her.

"Supper will be served within the hour."

"I will let them know."

Cal opened the door and walked into the parlour.

"Hello again, gentlemen. I hope you have whatever you need here?"

"We do. Somehow you have provided the best of what each of us prefer to imbibe." Dr. Franklyn saluted her with his glass.

"Thank you, we're fine. If you will give us some privacy, we have expedition business to discuss." Dr. Gostan turned away from her to Prof. Orthin, who ignored him.

"I am a member of the expedition. Lord Carroway specified I was to accompany you and record what you find."

"Stuff and nonsense, no slip of girl belongs on a voyage of science." Dr. Gostan looked like he might throw his glass at her.

"Nevertheless." Cal kept her gaze even and refused to let her hands shake. "I believe my father is the one who makes those decisions."

"A scientist should have a more open mind." Lahdin swirled his glass, then put it on the sideboard. "If Sir Shillingsworth has signed her up, then we will have to learn to get along." Lahdin dressed more like a labourer than a scientist, and refused any title attached to his name.

"Well, I for one will have nothing to do with this. If you go along, I will stay ashore." Dr. Gostan looked around for support. The others stepped away from him.

"I will instruct Hans to bring your luggage down, I'm relieved to have discovered your attitude before we set sail." Sir Shillingsworth entered the room, closing the door behind him.

Dr. Gostan sputtered, then slammed his glass on the table, slopping the drink across the dark wood.

"You are choosing this...girl, over a learned man?" He pointed at her with a shaking hand as if she were a criminal in the dock.

"I am dismissing someone who is insubordinate."

Cal shivered. Her father's voice had to have dropped the temperature in the room several degrees. Dr. Gostan deflated. He opened his mouth then sighed. The door closed behind him and silence filled the room.

"I will be delighted to have you along." Prof. Orthin smiled at her. "What is your specialty?" His shock of white hair and wrinkled face contrasted with his apparently boundless energy. When he looked at Cal, she felt his eyes had taken in every detail of her appearance.

"I'm an artist, Sir."

"You are the creator of that extraordinary portrait Lord Carroway has hung in his hall. You have seen below the exterior to show what he thinks he should be."

Cal blushed, oddly touched by his praise.

"As a scientist, I was trained to draw what I had seen. As an art lover, I know my best efforts are scribbles. I think you will be a welcome addition to our team." Dr. Franklyn bowed slightly in her direction. "What do you prefer to use for your art?"

"Pencil on paper is most accurate. A hard lead for fine work like schematics, softer for shading. Colour is nice, but not as portable."

"That is true." Lahdin wandered over. "I dabbled with oils in my youth, I was forever either setting up or taking down my easel."

"One could try watercolour, but that is a mystery to me." Dr. Franklyn shook his head. "One of my daughters paints watercolours of flowers and birds. Beautiful, but not scientifically accurate."

"Sounds lovely," Cal said. "What does she use to fix the paper so it doesn't smudge?"

"I have no idea if she uses anything at all. I imagine smudging would be a problem with pencil, I know what my journals look like after a few weeks in the field."

"I have a device I use to spray a fine coat of varnish on the paper. It keeps the picture safe from most handling. The drawback is the varnish takes considerable time to dry, so I only use it on occasion."

"That sounds like a useful thing to have. Where did you find such a thing?"

Cal looked down and fumbled for words.

"My daughter is being modest. She invented the device herself using her mother's perfume atomizer as a model." Sir Shillingsworth put a hand on her shoulder before venturing over to the sideboard to get a drink.

"You wouldn't believe how many tries it took to get a nozzle which would spray finely and evenly and not clog up immediately."

"I imagine you need to thin the varnish."

"Exactly, but too much and it doesn't do the job, not enough and the nozzle clogs."

Pentam entered the room and scanned across it before joining Sir Shillingsworth at the sideboard.

"I thought we had four scientists on the team?" He poured a glass of wine and took a sip.

"Dr. Gostan had a change of mind." Sir Shillingsworth stated flatly.

"Would you like me to look for another chemist? There may be someone at the university."

"I'm sure you will do admirably in his place, Pentam. If I recall it was one of your better subjects."

"Sir, those were undergrad courses..." Pentam trailed off as Sir Shillingsworth looked at him with a raised eyebrow. "I will make sure I refresh myself on the particulars. The equipment Dr. Gostan wanted has already been ordered and will be delivered to the ship within the week."

"Supper is served." Beth put her head in the door.

"Come, we eat, then we work." Sir Shillingsworth led them to the dining room.

***

Pentam sat up in his room reading his chemistry notes. The equipment wasn't a full lab, by any stretch, but it should be enough to identify chemicals they came across in their work. Anything beyond his or the lab's ability, they would bring samples back for the university. Even the things he did work on would be checked by the university chemists.

This could make or break his ambition. Too many mistakes, and no one would trust him with anything. It didn't matter he'd been dropped in at the last minute. The scientific community had no mercy.

Having a lab on the ship would make it easier to set up a darkroom for the photography. He had yet to tell Sir Shillingsworth he wanted to bring the camera. Appearing to compete with Cal for the work of recording the expedition would not please his mentor. Given the limitations of the camera, he'd have to stick with shots of specimens which could be held still for the necessary time.

Unless he could come up with a lighting source.

He turned down the lamp on his desk and turned in. They'd be travelling to the port in a few days.

Chapter 4 Boarding the Peregrine

Cal woke in the hotel room and stretched. She reached out and touched the log which lay on the table beside her bed. It was real. Today was the final day before they boarded the Peregrine and set sail to the west.

Over the past week, Sir Shillingsworth had been training her how to keep the log to his exacting standards. The task delighted her; it gave her reason to talk to everyone on the team about what they'd been doing. The endless penmanship lessons with Miss DeBantiche were finally paying off.

After breakfast with Sir Shillingsworth, Cal headed down to the dock. She'd packed one decent dress for any events which might call for more formality. The rest were dresses she'd added pockets to in order to keep her various supplies at hand. None of the men, neither scientists nor their assistants, made any comment, except Dan, Lahdin's assistant, who asked her to sew extra pockets on his shirts. She found a tailor for him instead, but took the request as a compliment.

The dock bustled with organized mayhem. Men carried boxes and barrels onto the ship. A group rolled two immense glass jars up the gangplank to the deck. Somewhere on the ship or the dock was the crate holding a ridiculous amount of paper, pencils, charcoal, even pens and ink. Lord Carroway had taken her list and added to it. Cal had been afraid there wouldn't be room on board for it all.

The HMSV Peregrine struck Cal as an odd name for a seafaring vessel, but she kept her opinion to herself. The Peregrine wasn't as large as she'd imagined. When she'd looked in the library to learn about ships, they all were huge things with crews of dozens of men.

Cal pulled out sketchbook and pencil and began to record the chaos on the dock. By the time her stomach informed her it was time for lunch, the movement on the dock had slowed to a crawl, but the ship still bustled with activity. She put away her materials and headed up to the hotel for lunch.

"Ah, there you are." Pentam waved at her. "Have your lunch, then we're going to meet at the dock."

"I'll make it quick." Cal ordered a light meal and sat with Dan. He wore one of his pocketed shirts.

"Each pocket has a different item I need to collect and preserve what insects we find." He took out and replaced a bewildering number of things.

"We'd better get on our way." Cal wiped her lips with the napkin. They went outside and joined the group walking down to the dock. Pentam met them there with the camera set up.

"I thought we could record the start of our journey." He pointed toward the Peregrine. "If you'll line up there with the ship in the background."

Dr. Franklyn looked uncertainly at Cal.

"Come on." She went to stand where Pentam pointed. "I've never been photographed before."

The others joined her and formed a ragged line. Sir Shillingsworth stood in the back, head and shoulders over Cal. Pentam moved them around until he was content with their arrangement.

"You need to hold as still as you can while I count to thirty." Pentam took something off the front of the camera and ran around to join the end of the line, counting slowly and steadily. He ran around as he reached thirty and replaced the cap on the lens.

"Thank you. I'll have a print for you later."

They wandered off in different directions. Cal headed toward the ship. A crewman stood at the dock end of the gangplank, wearing white clothes and looking not much older than Cal. His shoulders and arms bulged against the cloth of his shirt.

"Is it alright if I go look on board?"

"Henrichs," the crewman shouted, "expedition member asking permission to board."

"Send her up." The response came from above.

Cal walked nervously up the gangplank, adjusting for the slight movement of the ship. Huge rope bumpers kept the Peregrine from rubbing on the dock.

"Welcome aboard." A woman in a sharp looking blue jacket came up and put her hand out. Cal shook it; the woman's grip was firmer than most men's.

"Thanks." Cal looked around. "I'm Calliope."

"I'm Henrichs. First Mate of the Peregrine. Let me show you around. It will be a pleasure to have another woman aboard. I'd thought at first to put you in with me, but I'm in and out of my berth at all hours. I have a spot for you under the bow which should suit. Watch your step." They stepped over a raised sill and walked along a short hall to a staircase which might as well have been a ladder. Cal followed her down and along another passageway.

Henrichs kept up a running commentary on the ship and what they were passing. The staircase was called a ladder, the hall a passageway. Cal had looked up the onboard directions, but Henrichs reminded her. At the end of the passageway, Henrichs opened a door into a room hardly bigger than Cal's closet at home.

"The bunk folds down at night, up during the day to give you some space to move. There's a press here for your clothes and space for your supplies. When we're underway, I'll show you how to find them."

"It looks delightful."

"You may change your mind after a month at sea." Henrichs led the way back up to the deck. "If you have any questions, or problems, talk to me."

"Thank you." Cal walked back down the gangplank, the sailor at the bottom taking her hand for the last few steps.

"You coming on this cruise?"

"That's right. Cal." She put out her hand. He wiped his hand on his pants as if he hadn't been just holding it.

"Sam." He grinned. "You should've heard Henrichs laying down the law. We were to be friendly and accommodating, but not forward. It will be a pleasure having you on board."

"Thank you, Sam." Cal walked back up the hill to the hotel.

***

At supper Pentam brought over a stiff piece of paper and showed it to Sir Shillingsworth. He looked at it carefully, then slid it over to Cal. Pentam opened his mouth as if to protest, but stayed silent.

There on the paper stood the expedition, ship in the background. The detail was exquisite, with some blurring in the distance or where something had moved. Pentam looked like he had a ghost around him. Cal stood in the front, a silly grin pasted on her face, hair tangled, and blurred by the breeze. She looked...Cal wasn't sure.

"It's amazing, Pentam. I'd take an eternity to put so much detail into a picture." She held her finger just above the group on the photo.

"It's very expensive." Sir Shillingsworth picked up his utensils again.

"I'd chip in to help." Cal poured herself a glass of water. "After all, my expenses are all covered by Lord Carroway. It's only fair."

Pentam turned red, then looked at Cal gratefully.

"Talk to Henrichs about where you can do the developing. You'll want to get some heavy black cloth." Sir Shillingsworth turned to his meal.

Neither Pentam or her father made a move toward the print. Cal slipped it into her journal.

After supper, Pentam found Cal in the lobby.

"Were you serious about helping to pay for the photography?"

"Of course, what do you need?"

"I have plenty of glass plates and paper, but I could use more chemicals to treat them."

Cal reached into her pocket and pulled out what her father had given her to spend. She hadn't had time to touch it.

"Here, will this be enough?"

Pentam's eyes bulged a bit.

"Y-yes." He took the money. "Thank you."

***

Pentam ran to the chemist shop, hoping the man was still there. He was in luck.

"Hello again, I'm going to buy some more of the chemicals for photography."

"Very good, Sir." The chemist laid out packages on the counter. "The proportions are the same as the first you bought. Don't mix up more than you need at any one time."

The bundle took most of what Cal had given him, but it meant he'd be able to use the camera a lot more as part of their work. He put the packages in his bag and walked back toward the hotel.

He thought she'd be upset about the camera. After all it would be easy to see how it competed for the work she was doing. Yet, of the whole team, she was the only one to be interested in it. He didn't understand. On the way back, he passed a glassworker's shop. In the window, the man had hung tiny lenses on chains. He knocked on the window.

"Yes?" The man opened the door a crack and peered at Pentam.

"How much are the small lenses in the window?"

"The brass mounts are two and five, the silver ten and five, the gold...."

"I'd like one of the brass. May I have the chain as well?"

"Sure, tell people where you bought it."

"I will." Pentam emptied his pockets of his own money and took the lens and chain, wrapped in soft leather.

He headed up to the hotel, not a penny left to him, but they shipped out tomorrow, money wouldn't be an issue for some time.

Cal sat in the lobby, with pencil and sketchbook, of course. Pentam walked over and sat beside her.

"I have your change," he said. "You won't believe how much this means to me."

"I can imagine what it would be like to run out of paper or pencils." Cal looked at him and smiled. "I'm glad to help out."

"Here's what's left of your money." Pentam handed it to Cal who dropped it into her pocket without looking at it. He wished he could be that casual about money. All through school he'd scraped and saved, making do with second best. Pentam squashed the resentment. She'd given it to him without reservation.

"Um..." Pentam's tongue tangled around the words he wanted to speak. "I saw this and thought you might like it." He handed her the leather package. "It's only brass, I couldn't afford the silver."

"Brass is much more sensible." Cal turned the lens around in her fingers. Used it to look at her sketch. "This is wonderful. Thank you."

41

"It will help you draw the very small creatures." Pentam relaxed a little. She liked it and wasn't insulted.

"I will keep it close." Cal put the chain over her head and let the lens dangle like a necklace. She put her hand on Pentam's shoulder for an instant. "Thank you. I much prefer to be friends given we're going to be on the same ship for quite some time." Picking up her pencil, she went back to sketching.

Strange things were going on in Pentam's stomach. He went up to his room and lay down to sleep, but the memory of her hand on his shoulder kept him awake.

***

In the morning, Pentam joined the team for breakfast on shore for the last time. They took a line of taxis down to the docks. Sailors hoisted trunks and bags and hauled them up the gangplank. Captain Cully welcomed them on board, uniform pressed and sharp as if he only just put it on. The sun and wind had browned him. He stood relaxed, but Cal watched his eyes take in everything going on around him.

They trooped up the gangplank and stood on the deck.

"Hey, Cal, let's go to the bow and watch from there."

42

"Sounds good." She took the inevitable sketchbook from her pocket and followed him forward.

A booming horn made them both jump and the deck began to vibrate.

A sailor pulled a rope up from the dock and coiled it on the deck.

"Hi Sam, it is OK if we watch from the bow?"

"Should be fine, Miss Cal."

When did she have the chance to learn this fellow's name? About Pentam's age, he stood taller and much more muscular. He had an open, friendly face framed by short dark hair.

"I'm Pentam." He stepped forward.

"Sorry, Sir, but I'm all over oil from the rope." Sam held up his hands, and indeed they were black.

"That's fine, no shame in well-earned grime." Pentam could have kicked himself. He sounded like a fatuous idiot. But Sam grinned and nodded at them before going off to another task. Other ships, both steam and sail, moved on the harbour. Nobody seemed to make any effort to get out of anyone's way, but there weren't any close calls.

The Peregrine cleared the headland and began to roll with the waves.

"I don't feel so good." Pentam took a deep breath and headed toward his berth. He had no intention of making Cal watch him being sick over the side of the ship.

***

When Pentam abruptly headed to the stern, he looked more than a bit green. Cal's stomach wasn't that happy either, but she stayed at the rail with her eyes fixed on the horizon until the queasiness faded.

"What'cha doing?" One of the crew, a tiny man covered in grease and soot, stood beside her.

"I'd read a cure for sea sickness and wished to try it out." Cal slid a bit to the side to get out of the finger of smoke blowing from the stack.

The man sniffed, removing his cap to wipe his bald head.

"S'blowing a bit hot." He nodded at Cal. "Y'want to see the engines, ask fer Monky."

Cal nodded at him and went back to looking at the horizon. Her fingers itched, so she went looking for somewhere to sit while she pulled out her sketchbook and charcoal and lost herself in drawing.

"I see you've met Monky."

Cal looked up to see Henrichs, and raised an eyebrow.

"Soot on your dress. The man tries, but his job keeps him black as an old pot most of the time."

Sure enough, a smudge of soot on the side of her dress stood out.

"That's nothing." Cal held up her hands. "When I get really focused I can be head to toe charcoal."

"Good to see someone not afraid of a little dirt."

Henrichs stood beside her watching the sea for something.

"You're Sir Shillingsworth's daughter."

"Yes." Cal paused her hands a moment. "You know him?"

"Was cabin boy on the ship, first time he went to sea. Studying some islands off the coast of Africa. Ran into pirates and had a hell of a fight. Your father is no slouch with a blade. By the time we'd run them off, only a few of us were fit to sail. T'was me, the captain, and the bosun. Shillingsworth lent a hand and we limped back to port. Captain Cully kept me on and before long I was his first mate."

"You've been at sea your whole life?" Cal put her hand over her mouth. "Forgive me, I shouldn't intrude."

Henrichs laughed and put her hand on Cal's shoulder.

"Not my whole life, I've got some in me yet." She walked off toward the bow calling an incomprehensible order to Sam.

Cal flipped the page in her sketchbook and began a new picture.

***

45

The sun slipped beneath the water. Cal put her sketchbook away as the crew lit running lights bow, stern and amidships. She returned to her tiny berth below decks. With the bed folded up she had just enough space to change her dress and tidy her hair. Maybe she should wear it short like Henrichs? Her father would die of embarrassment. She tidied up the tangle from the wind.

She opened the door to a knock. Her father stood in the passageway swaying with unconscious grace. He held out something in his hand.

Cal took it but couldn't see well enough to know any more than it was a leather satchel.

"Bring it with you." Sir Shillingsworth headed toward the mess.

Cal slung it over her shoulder and followed him.

Captain Cully already sat with Pentam and the other scientists. Pentam no longer looked green as he laughed at something the captain said. Cal took a seat on a bench and examined the table. It had a ledge running the perimeter. Table and bench were bolted firmly to the floor. Gas lamps gave the stark grey walls something of a cheery glow.

"Welcome aboard." Captain Cully waved at Cal and Sir Shillingsworth, then looked around the room. "Just to keep things clear, Sir Shillingsworth is your boss. You do what he says. I'm your captain, mostly I'll leave you alone, but if I or my mate give you an order, we don't want any argument. If we're telling you what to do, it will be a matter of life and death." He relaxed and waved toward the galley. "Tea's hot, there's sugar and milk, but after today, just the sugar. You're welcome to fetch yourself tea at any time, night or day. Just don't hassle the cook or you'll find yourself peeling potatoes, he isn't as forgiving as I am.

"Sir Shillingsworth will show you the room I've set aside for you to gather and work. There's lockers to stow equipment. Never leave anything breakable loose, even on calm seas. You have a question about anything, ask the closest member of the crew. Now, you're scientists, the only thing in creation with more curiosity than cats, so explore the ship. If a crewman tells you something is dangerous, believe them. That's a lot easier than putting you back together. My purser is also decent at helping with sickness and injury, so talk to him if you need." He stepped back and sat down, resuming his conversation with Pentam.

Cal took the leather bag off her shoulder and put it on the table. Made of soft leather, it would hold her largest sketchbooks. When she opened it, the flap of the satchel had been sewn with loops the exact size to hold pencils, dozens of them. The main part of the satchel was divided into slots for sketchbooks and spaces for rolls of paper. A thin board gave the bag stiffness, but could slide out to draw on. One compartment held a roll of leather. When she examined it, she found it held ribs for charcoal sticks so they wouldn't break.

"You like it?" Sir Shillingsworth sat beside her with an odd expression on his face. Doubt.

"It's marvellous." Cal ran her hand over the leather. "I can't wait to load it with supplies."

"I thought you might need a bit more carrying space than your pockets for this trip." He tried a smile, but it came out a bit crooked.

Cal looked around the mess. The others were deep in conversation, waving tea cups and sloshing tea at each other.

"Do I thank Sir Shillingsworth, or my father?" Cal grinned at him.

"A little of both," he said.

"Well then, Sir Shillingsworth, thank you for the most wonderful and thoughtful gift." She threw her arms around him. "Thanks, Father. It means the world to me."

He relaxed and patted her back, not even pushing her away.

"What's up?" She raised her eyebrow at her father. "I love this, but you're acting strange."

"I never had the chance to bring your mother along on an expedition. She had a brilliant mind and helped write all my papers. But she always chose to stay with you." He reached out and touched Cal's cheek. "I'm glad she did, but then..." He sank into silence.

"I miss her too, Father, but nothing made her happier than talking about your work. I grew up looking at maps where you travelled, imagining camels and lions, blizzards and bears."

"I never knew that." Sir Shillingsworth sighed and kissed her hair. "I am glad you're here."

The animated discussion on the other side of the room continued.

"I made sure we have plenty of nets of various weights." Pentam looked in his cup and put it down.

"Netting is all very well, but we may need something more aggressive if any of the tales of sea serpents are true." Prof. Orthin waved his hands, making the others hold their cups out of the way.

"Since all we have are rumours and legends." Lahdin leaned back with sigh. "I fully expect all of our plans will be for nought, until we see the creature for ourselves."

"Very true," Pentam said. "But it is up to us to have the raw materials for any situation. We have everything short of a cannon to work with."

"We must hope for the best then." Dr. Franklyn slapped Pentam on the shoulder. "That we both see the beast, and have what we need to capture it. Yet capturing it will only be the beginning of our work. We will need to determine proper taxonomy."

"From the description, I expect we will find it to be related to the snake family, like the giant snakes in tropical jungles in the east." Prof. Orthin leaned forward.

"Determining taxonomy from sight is just asking for a later expedition to correct you." Lahdin chuckled and waved his hand. "I have some experience with that."

"Don't we all." Dr. Franklyn sipped at the remains in his cup. "It is the reality of being first, we always risk being wrong."

"Science is about being wrong, so we get closer to being right." Prof. Orthin put his cup down with a bang. "Now, I must head off to sleep to keep my mind sharp."

Cal nodded at Pentam as he collected the cups, then headed to her berth. Sleep sounded like a grand idea.

Chapter 5 Sailing the Briny Blue

After the second day of exploring the Peregrine, Cal
decided being at sea was boring. No, she had to be
exact. Being at sea with no responsibility was
boring. The scientists worked in what they called
the lab, calibrating instruments and exchanging
theories. Pentam set his darkroom up in a space
near the stern of the ship. He said it still had clips
for mops on the walls. Sir Shillingsworth double
checked the cargo, especially the giant glass jars,
now filled with preserving fluid for the sea serpent
they were to bring back. It would have to be a
very small sea serpent. She struggled every day to
find something to record in the expedition log.

Cal went looking for Monky.

The engine room might as well have had a sign
above it: *Abandon all hope, ye who enter here.*
Heat and noise struck like something out of the
Inferno. She stepped through the door and put her
fingers in her ears.

"Try this, Missy." Monky held out his hand with two bits of waxed cotton. She used them to plug her ears and the sound became bearable.

"So, tell me about this engine." Cal turned in a circle to take in the whole room. It made the little steam engine on the carriage at home look like a child's toy.

"Over here's the boiler." He pointed at a huge tank. "She's set exactly over the keel. Big as any locomotive. Coal's in the hold there, and water comes from further to the bow." He pointed at valves and pipes. "The coal we still shovel."

Cal followed him about the confined space, ducking under pipes.

"Here's the pressure gauge. Watch it close. Gets to sixty and we slack off the heat. Too much heat, a valve blows and she'll punch a hole through the hull. Needs fair bit more than sixty for that to happen." He crawled through to where huge pistons banged arms up and down turning a giant shaft which disappeared into the stern hull. She recognized similarities to the engine of their steam carriage, only immensely bigger. "That box keeps the seawater from coming in. It all looks simple, but ye got to be on your toes to keep her running smooth. Over here is the way we communicate with the bridge. The bells tell us the speed, four for full, three for three quarters and so on. A long and a short is for reverse." He pointed over to a

long lever. "That's the reverse, but the Cap'n wouldn't thank me fer demonstrating."

"Thanks for the tour." Cal climbed out the door and pulled the wax plugs from her ears once the deafening sound faded. A couple of the sailors she passed gave her odd looks. Pentam saw her as she came out on the deck.

"Not what I expect Sir Shillingsworth would want his daughter about." Pentam frowned and rubbed a finger gently across her cheek, then held it up, black with grease.

Cal ran to her berth and looked in the mirror, then laughed at the black streaked face staring back at her. She used a cloth to get most of the grease off.

Sixty psi felt like an awfully low pressure. The boiler would stand up to much more than that. Lines and curves floated in her mind. With higher pressure, it would be more efficient and turn the shaft faster. Not too fast; she imagined it shearing off and flying about the engine room. She'd ask how big the prop was, it would tell her how much stress the shaft took. She'd tried to draw these things, but they didn't come out as anything recognizable. Cal never tried explaining it. Her father already despaired of her.

After that she spent most of her time in the bowels of the ship, shovelling coal, adjusting valves, greasing gears and bearings. She avoided Pentam, who apparently was more determined than her father she be ladylike.

"By the time yer ashore, ye'll be a regular grease monkey." Monky grinned and Cal smiled at him before heading up to the deck, where again Pentam accosted her to express his displeasure.

"Until Sir Shillingsworth orders me to stay out of the engine room, I will continue to learn from Monky." Cal glared at Pentam. She wore a sailor's uniform begged from Henrichs as it was much safer than her dress in the engine room.

There was a knock on the door as she finished wiping the oil and grease from her hands and face. The uniform she put in a cubby away from her other clothes. The cap she wore kept the worst of the grease and oil out of her hair, but there were times she envied Monky his bald pate.

"Just a minute," she called out and pulled a dress over her head. When she opened the door, Sir Shillingsworth waited for her in the passageway.

"Join me for tea, in the mess." He might have worn the slightest of frowns.

She followed him up to the mess and sat in the corner while he fetched two cups of tea. He pushed one over to her.

"We'll be stopping at Finches Harbour to take on supplies. I'd like you on the deck to record the island and city. It is time to get serious. No more playing in the engine room."

Cal opened her mouth to argue that she wasn't playing, but closed it. This was Sir Shillingsworth talking, not her father.

"Yes, Sir." She cupped her hands around the tea. "Where do you suggest I take up position?"

Sir Shillingsworth stilled for a moment as if adjusting what he planned to say next.

"I think at the bow; you'll be able to move down either side of the ship at need." He took a sip of the tea and shuddered. "I will never get used to the taste of tea without milk. I want you to think about what you wish to do with your life."

The sudden shift in topic made Cal's head spin. She took a long sip to give herself time to think.

"I'm honestly not sure." She looked around the mess. "Some days I want to explore the world like you do, drawing what I see, so everyone can share the adventure. Other times, I want what I had with mother at home. Safe, familiar."

"You aren't planning to be an engineer?" He raised his eyebrow and she couldn't tell if he was teasing or serious.

"The engine is fascinating. It is so much more complex than the steam carriage at home. All those parts working in balance to push the Peregrine through the water. It's like a symphony in my head. But as interesting as it might be, I don't think a career as a grease monkey is for me."

Sir Shillingsworth let out a long sigh, and Cal laughed.

"You seriously thought I could be an engineer?"

"Could? Cal, you could be anything in this world. Should? Where are your gifts best used? Don't make up your mind too quickly. You don't want to limit yourself."

He put his hand on her shoulder, then carried his still full cup to the galley. Cal sighed and finished her tea, then headed for her berth. She needed to get organized to record their landfall at Finches Harbour.

Chapter 6 Landfall

In the morning, Pentam saw Cal on the deck with her satchel, and nodded to himself. He had been worried about her in that engine room. They were dangerous places, unsuitable for a woman of Cal's breeding.

Captain Cully had said they were to make landfall today at Finches Harbour. It would give them a day or two to spend time off the ship and pick up anything they were running short of.

Birds flew over the water, the first he'd seen since they'd left sight of land at home. They looked like the same species, but they were too far away for him to see details. The number and variety of birds increased through the morning. Straight ahead Pentam saw a faint cloud rising out of the water.

"Land ho!" came the shout from the top deck.

One of the birds landed on the railing near Cal and her fingers almost blurred as she drew the bird. He'd ask to see the picture later, if she was still talking to him.

By the time dinner was served in the mess the mountains rising out of the ocean were clear in the distance. Pentam rushed through his meal to get back out on deck, but was still slower than Cal. He stalked over to the stern to get away from her and try to think. The sight of dolphins playing in their wake mesmerized him.

After watching for a bit, he found Cal at the bow.

"Cal, there are dolphins playing off the stern, you might want to see them." Pentam wasn't sure about her reaction, but she flashed him a bright smile and hurried to the stern with her sketchbook. Pentam followed her and leaned against the rail while she filled page after page with drawings. He tried to recall the last time they'd simply been in each other's company without concern or plan.

Maybe I should try to do this more often.

As the Peregrine entered the harbour, the deck bustled as the crew prepared to dock. They politely, but firmly requested Pentam and Cal to locate themselves somewhere out of the way.

Once docked, Henrichs met the scientists at the gangplank.

"Most of you have been, if not here, in some other foreign land. I will remind you anyway. This is not home. The laws and rules of polite society are different. If you stay near the hotel, you'll be fine. If you want to wander further abroad, take advantage of the native guides the hotel employs. Money is different; again, at the hotel, there will be little problem; in the rest of the city, it may be. Under no circumstance are you to leave the city. No matter what the guide may promise, outside this city, we have no influence. Not every citizen of this country is happy with our presence."

"Thank you, Henrichs." Sir Shillingsworth looked at each member of the team waiting them to nod in acknowledgement. "If you want to spend a portion of your money here, see me before you disembark. I will add to Henrich's comments. If you plan on drinking, do it in the hotel bar. It may not be as exotic as other places, but it is safer. I don't want to waste time extricating anyone from trouble." He stepped to the side. Dan and Cal waited at Sir Shillingsworth's side until the others had left.

"I wouldn't mind a bit to spend while I'm here." Dan shuffled his feet.

"I've never had the chance to spend money I earned myself." Cal blushed and looked down.

"Follow me." Sir Shillingsworth led them away. They returned a few minutes later and disembarked.

"It might be wise if one of us remained on the ship." Pentam leaned on the railing watching the team vanish into two-wheeled carts pulled by muscular young men.

"You volunteering?" Sir Shillingsworth looked at Pentam sharply.

"I have some thinking to do." Pentam sighed and turned back toward the harbour.

"I see, very well. If you change your mind, I will take your place tomorrow. We will be here two nights." Sir Shillingsworth started down the gangplank then turned to Pentam.

"This might be a chance to make more use of that camera of yours."

Pentam fetched his camera and took photos of the scenic city curled along the shores of the harbour, mountains soaring in the background. When he thought he'd taken sufficient pictures to record Finches Harbour, he moved to the dock and got several shots of the Peregrine from different angles.

After developing the negative plates, he left them to dry and headed to the berth he shared with Matt, Prof. Orthin's assistant. There was a paper on his bunk. He picked it up and turned it over.

Cal had sketched him leaning against the rail watching the dolphins play in the background. The wind played with his hair and the sun lit half his face, leaving the rest in shadow. Somehow he looked strong, competent, at peace with who he was. Staring at the drawing Pentam began to understand Lord Carroway's reaction to her portrait of him. This was the person he imagined being when he wasn't confused by ambition or envy.

He lay on the bunk and studied the drawing until he fell asleep.

***

Cal sat in the two-wheeled taxi twisting her head as she tried to take in everything at once. She was happy Dan sat beside her. Henrichs' speech made her nervous, which she guessed was the point.

They pulled up in front of the hotel, a building which lifted bright and airy above them. Balconies dotted the face of the building. The pink stone was something she'd never seen before. It wasn't as smooth as marble. She checked into a room and immediately investigated the washroom. It had a wash stand and large bath. Cal rang the bell for service and asked the girl who responded for water for a bath.

"I send up men with water, then wait with you while they fill the bath."

"That's all right, I'm sure they won't bother me."

"Pardon, Miss, but is for their protection too." Her lovely dark skin grew darker.

"I understand, thank you for your consideration."

True to her promise the girl came up followed by a man carrying a bucket with great care. Another followed, then another until the bath was three-quarters full.

"What's your name?" Cal asked the girl while they waited.

"Meireka, Miss." The girl ducked her head.

"Please call me Miss Cal." Cal smiled at Meireka. "It will help me know you are talking to me, not some other Miss."

"Very good, Miss Cal." The girl bobbed in a brief curtsey.

"Tell me a little about your city." Cal turned to look out the window. A door to her right let out onto a balcony.

"We are blessed to live in beautiful place. The rains are plenty. Lots of flowers and birds. You see in morning. Lots of ships come here, bring wonderful things, and take away wonderful things. I live up there." Meireka pointed up toward the mountain. "My daughter is happy, and we eat well because of the work I do here. My man works on the mountain."

Cal looked at Meireka and tried to imagine her having a daughter. She didn't look old enough.

"What's it like being a mother?"

"Is most lovely thing. A smile on Cericia's face is worth more than gold. She has learned to walk and keeps her grandmother chasing her from morning to night." Meireka's face crumpled. "I miss her every day, but if she is to go to school, I need money to pay. We play in the evening."

"Your bath is ready, Miss." One last man stood in the doorway and bowed to her.

"I leave you now." Meireka curtseyed again.

"May I give you and the men something for your trouble?"

"If you please, Miss Cal."

Cal pulled some of her money from her pocket and peered at it. She had no idea what would be appropriate. She thought there were at least three men, and Meireka. A sovereign was the largest coin in her hand. Cal handed it to Meireka.

"Please share this with your co-workers."

Meireka's eyes went wide as she stared at the coin in her hand.

"Is too much for a bath." Her hands were shaking.

Cal took the young woman's hands.

"I would pay gold for a bath right now. It is not too much for me to give."

"Thank you, thank you, Miss Cal." Meireka's fingers closed around the coin. "You need anything you call." She gave a deep curtsey, then left the room.

Cal stripped all her clothes off, sank into the bath and sighed. For a long time, she lay in the water staring at the tiled ceiling. The water started to chill before she took the soap and scrubbed away at the accumulation of grease and grime.

Reluctantly, she climbed out of the bath and dried off. She found a dressing gown and wrapped herself in it then sat at the window. Even in that time the sky darkened.

A gentle knock at the door disturbed her reverie. Cal wrapped the robe tighter around her. She opened the door and saw an older woman.

"Do you have any clothes you wish cleaned, Lady Cal?"

Cal's lips twitched at her promotion. Maybe a sovereign had been a little excessive.

"I do." She gathered up her dress and other clothes which she'd scattered across the bathroom in her rush to get into the bath. Cal carried the bundle over to the woman. "Here, my thanks."

The woman handed her a folded bundle in exchange.

"Meireka said these should fit you. You can't wear a bathrobe to supper."

"You are most kind." Cal took the bundle. The women bobbed and vanished down the hall with the dirty clothes. Closing the door, Cal unfolded the bundle. It turned out to be a long skirt of some incredibly soft, light material. A white underskirt felt even softer under her fingers. Embroidery ran around the skirt's hem and waist. Flowers and birds in bright colours. The blouse was a match to the skirt with a gossamer light shirt to wear beneath. Cal dressed quickly, then admired the effect in the mirror. She spent more time than usual on her hair, trying to get it to suit what she wore.

Yet another knock at the door.

Cal opened it to see a man frowning at her. He wore a white suit which showed off his swarthy complexion. His coal black hair was oiled or waxed into place.

"One of the staff tried to change this into smaller coins." He held out the sovereign.

"I gave it to Meireka to share with the men who brought my bath water up the stairs."

The man looked a little uncertainly at her.

"It is a lot of money, Miss."

"Miss Shillingsworth," Cal said. "Sir Shillingsworth's daughter. I am here with the scientific expedition."

The man's discomfort grew.

"But Miss, you can't—"

"Miss Shillingsworth." Cal shocked herself with how much like her father she sounded. "And I will give what I please, if this upsets you, I will return to my ship."

The man paled, then wilted in front of her.

"My apologies, Miss Shillingsworth, but I have already sent the girl home. It is most unfortunate."

"It is indeed. Call a carriage and we will go and rectify your mistake."

"But... I can't... you can't..." the man stuttered and looked terrified. "It is night, it won't be safe for a Lady to travel up the mountain."

"Do you not have men in your employ who can accompany us and keep us safe?"

"I will arrange it immediately, Lady." He turned and almost ran away down the hall.

Cal picked up her satchel and followed him at a sedate pace.

Her father sat in a chair in the lobby.

"I saw the manager run past yelling for the bellhop to call a carriage and get four men to accompany the lady out. That wouldn't be you?"

"There was a misunderstanding the manager is going to fix."

Sir Shillingsworth nodded.

"I think I shall come with you."

"Thank you, Father. Your support means a great deal to me."

He stood up and put his arm out for Cal.

"If you are going to be a Lady, you must act the part."

Cal put her hand on his arm and they walked to the front of the hotel where a carriage waited. The men who'd carried the water to her room stood at each corner of the carriage. They bowed to her, and Cal smiled to them. The manager came out.

"Please, reconsider." He saw Sir Shillingsworth and bowed his head. "Be careful."

"I think you misunderstood." Cal pushed the burn in her gut down and kept her voice polite. "You will accompany us, explain to Meireka the nature of your mistake and return her money to her."

"As you will, Lady."

Sir Shillingsworth helped Cal into the carriage, then climbed in after her, followed by the manager with a look of misery on his face.

They started off slowly to allow the men to keep pace with the carriage.

"I must say, those clothes suit you, my dear. Not what the fashion is at home, but you could set a trend."

"Thank you, Father. Meireka had them sent up for me." Tears pricked at Cal's eyes. Now they were moving, her anger drained away leaving only sadness for the trouble she'd caused.

"Do you remember, the day when I came home to find you playing with a young boy?"

"Francis, I do indeed. We met on a shopping trip with mother and I invited him back to visit. As I recall we were covered from head to toe in mud from the garden."

"Yes, a most riveting sight. I remember being less than kind to the young man."

"Less than kind? Father, you threatened him with arrest and all kinds of misery. He was terrified. I infuriated you worse, by wrapping my arms around him and defending him. You ran him off anyway. I always wondered what happened to him."

"He is a blacksmith's apprentice. Soon after that incident his family moved across town. It took me months to find him. I had to apologize to his father, then his mother, his brother, his sister and placate the dog before they'd let me speak to him. I think having me apologize for my behaviour scared him worse than my yelling at him in the first place. I invited him to visit, but he wasn't comfortable. I kept track of him and when his father died, I made sure he would learn a trade to support his family. He named his daughter Calliope."

"Poor girl. Why didn't you ever tell me?"

"I guess I was too embarrassed, first that I treated your friend so badly, but after a while that I hadn't told you the rest of the story. I went off on one of my voyages and it never came up again."

Cal put her hand on her father's hand.

"Thank you for telling me. It might be silly, but there are still days when I dream about what it would have been like to have a friend of my own like him."

"It isn't silly, it is a sign of your great heart."

Cal giggled. "I can just imagine you facing down the whole family, and a dog?"

"Few things have terrified me more, but it taught me a truly essential lesson. No one is above making mistakes, and no one above the need to apologize."

"I was what, seven or eight? I can't believe you took it so seriously."

"I took it seriously *because* you were seven or eight. I just wish I'd told you sooner."

"Another lesson learned?" Cal looked over at her father and was shocked to discover his eyes glistening with unshed tears.

"All that I am, I've learned from your mother, and now you. She'd be proud of the young lady you've become." He reached over to caress her cheek.

"I thought I told you, I was no lady." Cal put her hand over his.

"Being a lady is about more than manners and a fancy dress."

They rode in silence as the homes on the sides of the street shrank and became more rickety.

"We approach Meireka's home." One of the men called from outside.

"He is Meireka's cousin." The manager spoke from across the carriage. "My name is Señor Amunda Calamphi." He bowed low in his seat. "It is my honour to have shared this ride with two such noble people."

The carriage stopped and Señor Calamphi climbed out, then waited like a footman for Sir Shillingsworth who helped Cal from the carriage.

An older version of Meireka came out to stare at them.

"Please announce to Meireka that Señor Calamphi has come to make amends for the mistake he made. It is inexcusable that I accused her without proof." Señor Calamphi looked at his feet.

The woman's eyes widened, but she called to her daughter in a liquid language. Meireka came out of the hut holding a toddler in her arms; her eyes red from crying.

"Señorita Meireka, I have made a terrible mistake, please accept my apologies." He placed the sovereign in her hand. "Forgive me."

Meireka looked at the coin in her hand, then at the manager, Cal and Sir Shillingsworth. She put her hand on the manager's arm. "I have my job?"

"You do."

"Please, stay. We have a little bread and fruit from the forest."

"We would be delighted." Cal's heart lifted. It would be all right after all.

One of the men ran off and returned with more people carrying food. Soon a celebratory party filled the street outside the hut. Cal stood to the side and sketched the people. Cericia babbled in delight, but soon fell asleep in her mother's arms. The picture of Meireka holding her daughter, looking down with tears of love on her face was one Cal wished she could capture in colour and hold for the rest of her life. She did what she could in pencil. As the party wound down, Cal tore the page from her sketchbook and handed it to Meireka.

"A gift for you and Cericia, so you never forget."

"I will never forget, Lady Cal. Never." Meireka tenderly stroked her daughter's face, then gazed at the drawing. "It is like a miracle. I never knew Señor Calamphi was such a brave and honourable man. I will see you tomorrow." She smiled brightly. "I knew those clothes would fit. My mother sews for a shop in the city. I hadn't delivered them yet."

"They are beautiful, you must tell me where the shop is. I would like to take more home. You may tell everyone Lady Shillingsworth will wear your mother's sewing on the streets of Anglia's capital."

Meireka leaned over and kissed Cal's cheek. "You are an angel."

Cal climbed back into the carriage followed by her father and Señor Calamphi. They rode down the hill, accompanied by the men. Cal's eyes grew heavy and she leaned against her father's shoulder and let them close.

***

Pentam woke and stretched. He put the drawing away carefully before wandering to the galley to see what he could scrounge for breakfast. Sir Shillingsworth sat at a table and waved Pentam over.

"Good morning, did you sleep well?"

"I did, Sir. I have some good shots of the harbour and the Peregrine."

"How did your thinking go?"

"I'm not sure, to be honest." Pentam sighed. "I seem to keep annoying Cal. I don't know why she puts up with me."

"She is an extraordinary young woman." Sir Shillingsworth smiled. "But I might be a little biased. Let her be who she is, and you be who you are. It's all you can do." He stood and patted Pentam's shoulder. "Go and see the city. It would be a shame to have visited and not seen anything of the place. Cal plans to go shopping, maybe you can accompany her." Sir Shillingsworth put a stack of coins on the table, then headed out to the deck.

Pentam shrugged, knowing that might as well have been an order. He picked up the coins and left for the hotel.

Cal was still eating breakfast with the scientists when Pentam arrived. She smiled brilliantly and waved him over. Pentam's heart flopped painfully.

"While we were sleeping, this young woman was out righting wrongs and seeing the sights." Lahdin pushed a sketchbook over to Pentam. He looked over at Cal, she nodded and he opened the book. Sketches showed people gathered around a fire. There was a lot of laughter. Sir Shillingsworth and another man stood out from the crowd, but both were clearly enjoying themselves. A great many sketches were of a young woman holding a little girl. They held a kind of glow as if Cal had trapped their obvious love on paper.

"These are amazing. There must be a story to go with them."

"Indeed, young Sir." The manager stood behind him. "She was kind enough to teach me a lesson in humility." He smiled and bowed in Cal's direction. "Would you be wanting anything to break your fast?"

"Thank you, but I ate on the ship, though it wasn't nearly as good as your food appears."

"Lady Cal, I've arranged for transportation for you for the day. Nothing as fancy as last night, that wouldn't be safe, but comfortable."

"Would you mind if I came along?" Pentam asked, his mouth suddenly dry. "I could carry your packages."

"You've been talking to Father." Cal shook her head. "I would be delighted to have your company."

"Really?" Pentam's voice squeaked and the men at the table laughed.

"Of course," Cal said. "You're good company when you aren't trying to make me into a lady."

Pentam stood and offered her his arm. Cal stood, arranged her satchel on her shoulder then took his arm. The scientists winked at him, then turned back to their meal.

The manager led them outside and pointed out a man with a two-seater cart.

"Joliu will take good care of you."

Pentam handed Cal up into the seat then clambered in after her.

Joliu took off without instruction, so Pentam figured Cal or the manager had already given instructions to the man. The way he kept a steady pace up and down hills impressed Pentam. He'd be out of puff walking, never mind jogging and pulling a cart.

The crowds edged out of their way. Once Joliu stopped to let a carriage pass. They arrived in a broad square filled with tents covering a bewildering variety of people selling an astonishingly diverse set of goods. There were things he could see immediately he would struggle to find in the capital city. Maybe it was the advantage of being a major stopping point for shipping to the west and south.

They wove through the market until Joliu pulled up in front of a store with a wooden front on the edge of the square.

"This is the store, Lady Cal."

"Thank you, Joliu. I may be a while. Find shade and water to drink while you wait."

"Yes, Lady Cal."

Pentam helped her off the cart then held his arm out.

"Lady Cal?" He looked sideways at her and caught her blushing.

"It's easier to let them call me what they will. I would only insult them by arguing."

"You'll have to tell me about it sometime." Pentam opened the door for her, then followed her into the shop. "But it suits you."

"Welcome, welcome." An old man bustled out from the back of the shop, bowing and smiling, stopping Cal from replying. "What may I interest you in?"

"Dresses, hats, scarves." Cal looked around the shop running her fingers across the fabrics. She pulled out a blouse in bright colours which would make her look like a jungle parrot. Pentam clamped his lips tight to keep the thought private. He spotted something hanging to one side of the shop, as if it were more decoration than something to be sold.

It resembled an Anglia gown, if one had been made of gossamer and cobwebs, then embroidered over every inch.

"Cal," Pentam pointed to the dress. "I'd love to see you in this."

Cal's eyes widened and she put down the blouse to come inspect it.

"Do you think it would fit me?" She inspected the embroidery with a wistful look on her face.

"Only one way to find out." Pentam couldn't keep the grin from his face. Cal frowned. "You did come looking to buy clothes. Why not buy the best?"

She nodded to herself, but glanced over at the dress, her hands twisted together.

"Señor." Cal turned to smile at the proprietor. "Is there a place I may try this on?"

"Only my humble room in the back, but is not fine enough."

"It will be all right." Cal lifted her chin.

The shopkeeper lifted the dress off its stand and laid it over her arm.

"Please, the back door can be barred, and your man can stand in the door here."

"My thanks." Cal handed Pentam her satchel and disappeared into the back. Pentam stood behind the counter with his back to the short hallway. The shopkeeper wandered through the store looking at his stock as if he'd never seen it before. He nodded a couple of times, but shook his head more.

"Pentam, what do you think? There's no mirror, so I don't know how it looks."

He turned to look and his jaw dropped.

"Good God, you'd set the city on fire in that dress."

"Is that good?" Cal lifted her arm. "I'm really not used to this kind of thing."

"You are beautiful."

"Stop joking around." Cal frowned at him.

"I wish I had my camera, then I could take a picture and show you." Pentam's heart pounded painfully.

"Lady, you are like an angel in my poor shop." The shopkeeper held out a broad brimmed hat. "Try this."

The hat added mystery to beauty. Pentam closed his eyes as if it was painful looking at her.

"That bad, Pentam?" He'd never heard Cal sound so unsure.

"You're like the sun, I can't look too long before I burn to ash."

"Oh, come on, now I know you're teasing."

"Wear that dress back to the hotel and if the rest of the team doesn't fall over themselves when you walk in, I'll eat my hat."

"And if they do?" Cal's voice was soft.

"You let me take your picture to show you."

"I guess I'm buying the dress." Cal looked at the shopkeeper. "How much?"

"For the Lady, three sovereigns." The shopkeeper looked like he was holding his breath. Pentam laughed at the look on the man's face when Cal looked at Pentam.

"My purse is in the satchel; would you pay the gentleman?"

"My Lady may keep the hat." Shopkeeper ran through his shop looking at and rejecting things until he came on a pair of white gloves. "Please, Lady, accept these as a gift and remember my shop kindly."

Cal took the gloves from him and looked helplessly at Pentam.

"I have no idea how to put them on."

Between Pentam and the shopkeeper they got the gloves on her hands and up her arms past her elbow. The shopkeeper had added a couple of scarves to the pile, then ducked into the back and retrieved the skirt and blouse. He wrapped everything carefully in paper and looked like he wanted to add more to the bundle.

"Thank you." Cal inclined her head. "It has been a pleasure to visit you."

"Please, if you return to our city, remember to visit."

"I will." Cal tilted her head and Pentam offered her his arm and walked her out of the shop. "All right, what's going on? I've never seen anyone react like that to me buying clothes."

"I think he expected you to bargain with him."

"Bargain? But I'd pay fifty pounds or more for a gown like this in the city."

"He probably thought you'd stalk out of the shop in anger when he said three sovereigns."

Cal giggled, and shook her head. "I appear to sow confusion wherever I go."

Joliu ran up and bowed deeply.

"Is Lady Cal ready to return to the hotel?"

"I would really like to look around the market more. I've hardly seen any of it."

"I don't know if that would be wise now." Pentam winced waiting for her reaction, but Cal looked down at herself and sighed.

"The hotel, thank you, Joliu."

Pentam helped Cal into the seat, then to arrange her skirts. He climbed up beside her, feeling grungy and underdressed next to this Lady.

"Let's go, Joliu." Pentam said.

The crowds parted for them as if Cal were royalty. They were almost out of the market, when Pentam made Joliu stop.

"Wait a moment, Lady Cal." He ran over to a booth and entered into a spirited bargaining session but got what he wanted for less than he'd hoped. The woman wrapped it up for him, and he dashed back to the cart. This might make up for his earlier gaffes, but it was so hard for him to see Cal differently from the society woman he'd met through her father.

"All set."

At the hotel, the staff scurried to help Cal off the cart, then held the door for her. Pentam carried his bundle, her package and her satchel. He'd convinced her it didn't go with the dress.

Señor Calamphi bowed deeply to Cal and led to a table in the lounge calling for the staff to bring some iced juice for the Lady.

Pentam sat beside her, resigned to being ignored, and not really minding.

The juice came and a young girl ran up with a fan to gently waft air across the Lady's face.

Lahdin walked into the lounge, noted Cal, then Pentam sitting beside her. His puzzlement turned to amazement and he ran out of the room. A few minutes later he returned, followed by the rest of the team. They stood in middle of the room staring at Cal. Prof. Orthin headed over to her.

"My dear, I am flabbergasted. I should have expected the daughter of Sir Shillingsworth to be a ravishing beauty, but ship life isn't conducive to such fine looks."

The others stood back nodding. Dan had turned red and was twisting his hands in front of him.

Sir Shillingsworth strolled into the lounge and over to Cal.

"Calliope, you are looking especially nice today. It's good to see you enjoying fine clothes." He nodded at Pentam, then herded the team off to another table.

"I believe you need to let me take your photo."

"All this over a dress?" Cal looked quizzically at Pentam. "This isn't very practical."

"Sometimes practicality must give way to beauty. Think of it as a work of art." Pentam's stomach hurt, he wasn't making things better.

"I'm still just me." Cal plucked at the sleeves. "And I'm no work of art."

82

"You can wear beautiful clothes and still be yourself." Pentam put his hand out, then pulled it back. "Let me take your picture, and you'll see."

Cal nodded reluctantly, then turned her attention to her drink.

Chapter 7 Back to Sea

Cal said her farewells to the staff at the hotel, promising again and again to return if she was back this way. Her father collected what little she still had in her room and said he'd meet her aboard ship.

She rode with Pentam down to the dock, then waited with Joliu while Pentam fetched his camera.

He set up on the dock first and took a couple of pictures with the Peregrine in the background. After that he led her up the gangplank and took a couple more with the harbour in the background.

"Stop, you're going to use up all your supplies on me."

"I have plenty," Pentam said, but he put the cap on the lens and carried the camera off.

"You look wonderful." Henrichs appeared at her side. "I'm guessing all your friends are acting strange and you don't know why."

"Exactly. I'm still me."

"True, but a pearl in an oyster shell is the same as the pearl set in a gold setting as a necklace. Today they've seen you in that gold setting."

"What happens when I go back to the oyster shell?" Cal waved at her gown. "I can hardly work wearing this."

"That all depends on you," Henrichs said. "Come, Captain Cully would like to see you before you return to the shell."

Henrichs guided her through a passageway to a section of the ship Cal had been told was the officer's quarters. Henrichs knocked on the door then opened it and ushered Cal in.

"Welcome, Cal, I like to have ladies for a chat and tea. Henrichs will join us to keep everything proper. I am remiss, I should have invited you as soon as you came aboard the Peregrine."

Captain Cully pulled out a chair and handed her tea in a fine china cup.

"I don't get to socialize like this very often, so it is a pleasure to have you visit. What did you think of your time on shore?"

They talked easily about the island and the city. Captain Cully was especially interested in the trip up the mountain and the shop.

"When you set the city on its ear, I will be the one who has a line on similar gowns for the

85

ladies who will be very happy to overpay for them." He grinned wolfishly.

When the sun touched the mountain top, Cal excused herself and headed to her berth. Getting down the ladder in her dress was a challenge but no one was watching so she tucked up the skirt and scurried down before straightening the gown. She had barely enough room in her berth to remove the gown, under-skirt and blouse. Strangely reluctant to put on her old pocketed-dress, she put on her one 'nice' dress. There was just enough room in the locker to hang up her gown. She had no idea what to do with the hat. The gloves she rolled off her arms and put with the hat.

Maybe she'd ask Henrichs if there was a place in cargo for her to store the outfit. She certainly didn't need it on board.

Pentam had dropped the bundle of her other clothes at the end of her berth. She unpacked it to put them away, putting the skirt and blouse with the gown. Then she noticed the other package.

Curiously she tugged the string off and pulled away the paper. Inside she discovered a pair of pants and a shirt made of sturdy material. There was a note in Pentam's handwriting.

Even a fine lady can't wear a gown to work in an engine room.

Cal laughed and hugged the pants and shirt to her. How could he be the one to insist she wear that dress; and also buy her these? Would he be upset if he knew she preferred the more practical clothes? She laughed so hard her legs buckled dropping her to the floor where the laughter somehow became tears, though she didn't have any idea why she was crying.

***

In the morning, Cal dressed in the pants and shirt and headed up for breakfast. The fires had been stoked and the ship vibrated. They'd be sailing soon.

She stopped a moment outside the mess, then squared her shoulders and walked in as if it was any other day. Prof Orthin waved at her. Dan smiled and Pentam slid over to make space for her.

"Not a fine gown, Lady Cal, but much more sensible for shipboard life." Pentam smiled at her.

"Thank you." Cal leaned over and kissed his cheek. "It is nice to have one who understands."

"I'm not sure I do." Pentam touched his cheek. "But I'm willing to trust that you know what you're doing."

Cal laughed. "I have no idea myself."

"You'll figure it out." Pentam slid a pile of paper over to her.

Cal hesitated, then turned over the first one, then the others, one after the other in quick succession.

"This can't be me." The woman in the picture stood comfortable and assured. The shadows from the hat made her face more interesting. The gown blurred slightly where the breeze moved it. It made the woman look ethereal, like an angel, like a lady.

"It's you." Pentam grinned, "there were no other stunningly beautiful ladies about."

"But how can I be this," Cal pointed at the photos. "and this?" She waved her hand over the pants and shirt.

"They are both you. You don't need to choose."

"Pentam, this is a gift beyond measure." Cal looked through photos again, slower this time. "These are brilliant. If I was looking at a painting or drawing, I'd be amazed at their vision and ability."

"The camera does the work." Pentam shrugged looking uncomfortable.

"No, it isn't the camera, it's the way you use the camera. See how the roughness of the hull contrasts with the dress. And the town in the background of this one looks like she's standing in the midst of lights. Your photos make me see the world differently. Thank you." Cal stood up and gathered the photos to hand to Pentam.

"No, those are yours. I made two sets of prints. It's the least I can do after all the help you've given me."

Cal put her hand on his shoulder. "I don't know how to thank you." She left him with an odd expression and went looking for Henrichs to arrange getting the gown and other fancy clothes stored safely.

Sir Shillingsworth saw her on the deck and laughed so hard Cal spun around to see if it was truly him.

"You look just as lovely as in that gown." He said when he regained control.

"Are you sure you didn't hit your head?" Cal peered at him.

"Let's just say I'm happy that you've kept yours. Captain Cully has told me it will be a week or two before we reach the Sargasso Sea. I hear Monky is missing your company."

"Thanks, Father." Cal scurried off to stash her satchel in her berth. She grabbed her earplugs and descended into the belly of the ship.

"Ah, Missy, good to have my helper back. You enjoy your shore time?"

"It was interesting."

"Always is, Missy, always is." He pointed over to the corner. "Grab the grease and give those bearings a dose while I adjust the water flow."

They worked through the day. Monky explained that starting and stopping the engine took extra care as the pressure could change rapidly.

The next few days, Cal was as happy as she could ever remember being. She pulled out the photos every night after she'd meticulously cleaned her hands.

Pentam had told her she didn't need to choose.

***

The ship shook and Cal considered checking it out, but nothing else happened so she relaxed. Sleep had barely reclaimed her when shouting woke Cal again. She threw a dress over her head and went out to make sure the ship wasn't sinking.

Monky and a crowd of sailors huddled around a moaning figure on the deck.

"Ye don't want to look, Missy. It ain't pretty." Monky stood between her and the huddle.

"What happened?"

"Was greasing the pistons when the ship took that bump. His arm got chewed up something awful."

Cal winced. The big pistons were nerve wracking to work near.

"Will he be all right?"

"Depends on what ye mean. The purser's coming t'look. He might live. Don't know if he'll want to."

"OK, back to work. I'll let you know as soon as there's something to know." Henrichs appeared on deck with the purser in tow.

"Monky, can you manage the engine room for now?"

"Not really, ma'am. I can barely stand straight."

"I can manage it." Cal stepped forward. "As long as we're just steaming straight on, I'll be fine. I won't do anything dangerous."

"All you do is watch the pressure. No grease, you don't go near the engine."

"No, ma'am."

"Off you go then." Henrichs sighed. "And thank you."

Cal changed her clothes, grabbed her ear plugs and headed down. The engine room, which felt exciting and welcoming with Monky at her elbow, clattered ominously like a monster gnashing its teeth. She straightened her shoulder and looked at the pressure. It was high; she opened the water valve to cool it off. Most of the night she alternated between adjusting the valve and stoking the fire. At some point, she realized she needed to back off on whatever she was doing before it reached the pressure she wanted. She slowed down and paid attention to the lines in her mind's eye showing the dance between heat and pressure. After that she relaxed into a calmer rhythm.

Monky startled her when he put a hand on her shoulder.

"Go sleep, Missy. Ye did fine."

Cal crawled up to her berth, and forced herself to clean up before she fell into her bunk and closed her eyes.

A knock on the door woke her. The light from the porthole suggested she'd slept at least partly through the day.

"Captain's compliments, but he'd like to see you on the bridge." Sam stood outside the door when she'd dressed and opened it.

"Am I in trouble?"

"Not for me to say, Miss." But he shook his head slightly and Cal's heart slowed down a little.

Sam led her up to the bridge. She'd never been up this ladder before. Sam knocked on the door.

"Miss Cal, Captain."

Cal walked onto the bridge, immediately distracted by the levers, wheels and other things; she couldn't guess their purpose.

"I hear I owe you a debt for keeping the engines running."

"How is he doing?"

"The purser gave him morphine and cleaned up the shoulder as best he could. He's not a surgeon. We have to wait now to see if it heals or infection sets in." Captain Cully leaned over a dial beside the large wheel and adjusted it slightly. The sailor holding it nodded.

"That's horrible."

"Going to sea is dangerous, Miss Cal. Accidents happen. We do our best to prevent them, but we shipped out with only two engineers. I'd hoped to find another at Finches Harbour, but no luck. Now we have one engineer." Captain Cully wiped his forehead and sighed.

"Two," Cal said. "Or at least one and a half."

Captain Cully nodded. "Sir Shillingsworth told me you'd respond so. You've seen the engine room is no playground. It's likely the most dangerous place on the ship."

"Monky's taught me to be careful. No loose clothing, think only about what you're doing at that moment. Stay aware all the time."

"He's a good engineer. If you feel you're up to it, I'd like you to take the first half of the night, six hours, no longer than you worked last night. I will cover the second half of the night myself. As Captain, I need to know every part of my ship. If you aren't able, I'll understand and take the full shift and Henrichs will step in as Captain."

"I would like to try, Sir." Cal looked at him. "I promise if it gets to be too much, I will tell you."

"I've appointed one of the men to train with Monky starting tomorrow, so we will have another man in the engine room. This will only be a temporary measure. Thank you, Cal. See the purser about your pay."

"Pay? My father is already paying me." Cal held up her hand.

"He is paying you as artist and expedition member. I will be paying you as apprentice engineer."

"I don't need the money." Cal's stomach twisted. It didn't feel right, but the Captain had a stubborn look on his face. "All right, sign me up, but I want you to pay all my wages to the man who was hurt last night. He'll need it more than I."

"Very well." Captain Cully smiled sadly. "We'll pray he lives to spend it. Dismissed."

The Captain turned back to the wheel—*the helm*, Cal corrected herself. She needed to be accurate now.

She went to fetch her earplugs and climbed down to talk to Monky.

"I'm fine, Missy. You go rest."

"In a minute." Cal pointed around the engine. "You've shown me enough to play at being an engineer. I need you to teach me the rest. I'll come down an hour before my shift starts and you tell me what I need to know."

"That I will." Monky pointed to the door. "Now, as yer superior officer, I'm ordering ye to stay rested. I won't have you hurt too."

Cal saluted and left the engine room.

She went to the bow to think. If she was going to run the engine room the first night shift, she'd be best to sleep in the afternoon, rising for supper before going down to work.

"Are you crazy?" Pentam stood with his back to the rail. "An experienced engineer gets injured and you volunteer to take his place? How are you going to draw with an arm missing, or worse?"

94

"If I don't, it could slow down the expedition."

"So what? If we take a little longer it doesn't matter." Pentam's face turned red.

"It does. We only have so much coal, so much water. The longer we take, the more likely we are to run out. You want to row back home?"

"We could go back to Finches Harbour and hire someone."

"The Captain tried, he couldn't find anyone." Cal stepped forward until she stood nose to nose with Pentam. "You told me I didn't need to choose, but now I have to choose, at least for a while. I'm choosing this." She wiped her hand on her pants and showed him the grease.

"You're impossible."

"Yes, I am. You should have talked to my father before trying to shape me into something else." She turned to look out over the ocean. "If you'll excuse me, I've been given orders to be rested for my first shift as the Peregrine's apprentice engineer. If you ask the purser, he'll show you where I signed up."

Pentam stomped off swearing under his breath. Cal tried a couple of his more colourful curses.

"I see you're studying the role of sailor seriously." Sir Shillingsworth stepped up beside her as Cal's face burned red. "I understand Pentam's concern, but what is more to the point, I trust you. If this is what you need to do, I will not argue."

"So I'm an engineer after all."

"Apprentice engineer." He put his hand on her shoulder. "Please be careful."

"I will, Father, you can be sure of it."

She watched the ocean for a while longer until the horizon stopped blurring and she didn't have to wipe her face.

Lunch was a silent and lonely meal as the rest of the team kept on with their plans and theories. Cal was crew now, outside the group. She left as soon as she'd finished.

Back in her berth, Cal packed the photos Pentam had given her away in a journal. She updated the log with the new situation. She'd made a habit of writing in the log every night before she slept. Now it was strange to do it with light streaming in the porthole.

Knocking at the door woke her. Cal sat up groggily.

"Supper is on, engineer." Sam called through the door. "Henrichs asked me to be sure you were awake as you're in the wrong part of the ship to hear the bells."

"Thanks, Sam."

Cal dressed and headed for the mess. She filled her plate and sat with Sam.

"How long have you been working at sea?"

"Me da was a sailor. Got hurt, not as bad as Adam, but bad enough he retired and opened a bar. Told mum he was an expert on bars. I went to sea that year as cabin boy on a coaster. A year back I signed onto the Peregrine. I'm still the youngest, but at least I'm not the boy no more."

"Wouldn't I be the youngest now?"

"Don't matter, Cal. You're an engineer, makes you more like an officer, but you work harder."

"I heard that, Sam." Henrichs called from a table behind them.

Sam ducked his head, but grinned at Cal. She grinned back. After supper, she picked up her earplugs and headed down.

"Ah, Cal." Monky waved her in. "This be Bran, he's learning the ropes, same as you." For the next hour Monky talked her through the boiler in detail, each valve, what they did and how to replace them. Mostly by emptying the boiler, cooling it off and hammering at it with a big wrench. "T'morrow's the engine itself."

They left Cal for the rest of her shift. Bran was taller than Cal and kept banging his head, but he stuck with it.

Through the night Cal watched the pressure and went over the boiler, naming each valve in turn. She spotted the one which was the equivalent of the pressure control valve on the steam carriage, but this was as big as her head.

Captain Cully came and relieved her and Cal climbed up to her berth to clean up and sleep.

Cal ate mostly with Sam. They played cards on the rare occasions he had a little extra time. The rest of the time, Cal sketched. She started at the bow and worked her way toward the stern, drawing the ship in the same way she created the schematic for Hans. When she ran out of ship she started drawing the engine room from memory, labelling each part as she went. As she drew, the pictures in her head showing stress and failure points grew clearer. Some of it didn't make sense, but whoever built it had to know what they were doing.

Pentam ignored her completely. The others greeted her, but they were busy on their own schedule.

The conversations with the crew were very different from the ones with the scientists, though they still centered around the goal of the expedition.

"Don't know that it's wise to be looking for a sea serpent." An older sailor glanced over at the scientists, still speculating about what they might find. "None of the stories say it's a good thing to see one."

"This is the modern age," Sam said. "Science is all about learning new things." He winked at Cal.

"Learnin's all well and good." The old sailor glared at Sam. "But it don't mean we can't be sensible. Somethin' hit the ship. It weren't no wave."

"Maybe it was a whale." Cal said.

"You seen any whales, Missy?"

Two weeks after the accident, Captain Cully told Cal she was being put back on reserve. That afternoon they buried the injured man at sea. Cal stood staring at the water heaving around them with her father's arm around her shoulder.

"Tomorrow, we enter the region of the Sargasso Sea." Sir Shillingsworth told her. "I need my artist on deck."

"She'll be there."

Chapter 8 The Sargasso Sea

Whatever Cal had expected of the Sargasso Sea, this wasn't it. The ocean spread wide and blue under a cloudless sky, only the slightest of swell disturbing the water. She swayed instinctively as she sketched.

"What are you sketching?" Dr. Franklyn came up behind her. "There is nothing to see." His white eyebrows lifted.

"That's what I'm sketching." Cal didn't turn to look at him.

"What?"

"Nothing." She held the sketchbook so he could see, then put the book away. "I'm supposed to record what we see and do." Cal put her hand up to shade her eyes and peered out over the water.

"At this point, the Sargasso Sea is mostly empty water with a few clumps of seaweed. As we get closer to the gyre, the clumps will get thicker and closer together. In some places, it may pose a hazard to the prop, but we'll see."

"The gyre?" Cal looked at him.

"Where the currents of the ocean circle and pull anything in the area together."

"Sounds dangerous."

Dr. Franklyn laughed. "It's nothing to worry about. It's huge, but not strong."

He clomped off down the port side of the Peregrine.

They sailed through the day. When the sun reached its zenith, she pulled a hat from her satchel and covered her head. The sun had dropped halfway to the horizon when excited voices rose to the starboard. Cal walked around the deck to where Dr. Franklyn and his assistant, Hank, pointed out over the water.

Far away, tiny shapes disturbed the calm surface. They got closer until Cal could tell they were fish with enormous fins, leaping out of the water to glide an astonishing distance before splashing back into the ocean.

Behind them, a single black fin broke the surface, then vanished. Cal's fingers flew across the paper, catching the grace of the flying fish and the ominous fin. As she drew, the pictures in her mind showed how the size of the fins related to how far they glided. The double vision could be annoying when she was only interested in recording the scene. Annoying or not, her fingers insisted on adding the equations.

They saw several schools of the fish, and one fish even landed in a lifeboat on the port side. Prof. Orthin clambered down to fetch it.

"I would like to get a photograph." Pentam leaned over the side. "And record it exactly for science."

"Very well." Prof Orthin grinned up at them. "You can take its picture, then I will dissect it before giving it to the cook. They are delicious."

Pentam took photos from every conceivable angle, even when cut open and splayed on the dissection table. Cal stood back and recorded the process in her sketchbook. Pentam only spoke to her to complain she was in his light.

"It is a common enough fish." Prof. Orthin delicately took the fish apart. "But it never hurts to check."

"Besides, it keeps you both in practice, and well fed." Dr. Franklyn leaned against a wall watching Pentam more than Prof. Orthin.

"Nothing wrong with that." Prof. Orthin didn't lift his head from his work.

Cal took the opportunity to inspect the lab, which she'd not had reason to explore previously. The dissection table took up one wall, comically huge for the tiny fish, but she imagined they'd need that size later. A collection of chemistry equipment was stowed on the wall opposite, over in the corner. Shelves lined another wall with boards holding books against possible heavy movement. Presses of different sizes were ready to preserve botanical samples. Jars with formaldehyde for animals.

The days continued in that manner, mostly empty ocean broken by glimpses of fish or other creatures. Cal spotted the first mat of seaweed and Captain swung the Peregrine to pass close by. The plants were brownish with white nodules acting as floats. Pentam hooked some up onto the deck for recording with his camera. A tiny crab scuttled across the deck before escaping over the side. Lahdin argued with Dan about whether it was a new species.

The mats grew closer and thicker until they were rarely out of sight of any. Several times they'd stopped while the boat was lowered for closer examination. Sir Shillingsworth kept careful track of who'd been out on the boat until they'd all had a chance.

Cal went out with Dr. Franklyn.

"It looks like a marsh." Cal scanned the mat.

"You'd be in trouble if you tried to walk on it." Dr. Franklyn pulled a weed up to look at then tossed it back. "It would let you drop through, but would very likely trap you underwater."

"So it is like a marsh—not quite water, not quite land."

"At least marsh has a bottom." Dr. Franklyn held out a strand of seaweed. "Sketch it quickly before it dries out."

***

Captain Cully sat beside Cal at the supper meal.

"How is the transition back to scientist working?"

"I'm no scientist, just an artist. I draw and let the scientists do the thinking." Cal spooned fish soup into her mouth.

Captain Cully laughed and attacked his own soup. "Back in the day of sail, ships would get caught out here. Not much wind, and the seaweed can gum up a rudder quick enough. You'd have noticed us going around, not through. Don't want to send a man over to clean the screw."

"It couldn't get thick enough to trap us, could it?"

"That's one question I'd rather we not answer the hard way. A ship this big is hard to row."

The captain finished his soup and left the mess as Monky walked in.

"Heh, Missy. How're things topside?" He fetched a mug of tea and sat across from her.

"Lots of seaweed and small creatures. Crabs mostly. I didn't know there were that many kinds of crab. Fish too, under the weeds. Prof. Orthin has a periscope he uses to look under water."

"So the trip's worth yer while?"

"I'm not doing much but sketching whatever they ask me to. Oh, I almost forgot." Cal dug through her satchel. "Here I thought you'd like this." She handed him a page from her sketchbook showing him beside the boiler. The fire glowed fiercely as he shoveled coal into its maw. "I wanted to thank you for teaching me about the engine."

"Well now." Monky held the paper by the edges. "Ain't nobody gave me art before." He peered at it closely as if memorizing it. "Could ye keep it safe for me, Missy? There's nowhere fer me to stow it." He handed the drawing back. "It should be me thanking you. Ye saved us a good bit of trouble. Did a right sweet job of it too."

Cal carefully replaced the paper in her satchel. "In the engine room you called me Cal, why have you gone back to Missy?"

"In the engine room, ye were Cal, apprentice engineer. Now, ye'r Missy, artist for the passengers. Two different people, see?"

Cal laughed and shook her head. "I'm still on call if you need me. I'll get the drawing back to you when we get home."

"Ye'r a wonderful lass. Me wee ones'll love t'see what their da does fer a livin'."

He finished his tea and nodded at her before leaving the mess. Cal looked at where he'd sat. She hadn't expected such a strong reaction to a simple sketch. It reminded her again of the gulf between the crew and the scientists.

For the next few days, Cal surreptitiously drew portraits of each of the crew at work. Sam tidying ropes on the deck. Bran checking the pressure in the engine room. When she'd finished, she started on the scientists. Dr. Franklyn poking at a clump of seaweed. Prof. Orthin bent over a fish on the dissecting table. Lahdin crouched on deck, eye to eye with a crab. The assistants too, who had specialties of their own. Sir Shillingsworth she drew in discussion with the scientists pointing away to the west.

The advantage of drawing portraits was her mind didn't keep trying to add numbers and equations in the margin.

As she put the last drawing in her journal for safe keeping, they arrived at a mat of seaweed which spanned as far as they could see to port or starboard.

Chapter 9 The Gyre

Captain Cully ordered the Peregrine to slow, then came down to the deck to consult with Sir Shillingsworth. Cal drew them as she listened.

"We can't sail through this stuff; it'll tangle the screw in no time. Won't be stuck out here."

"I have every intention of reporting back to Lord Carroway. This is your ship, Captain Cully. We'll turn north or south from here."

"We turn north then, sail against the current and cover more of the mat."

"North it is." Sir Shillingsworth looked over at Cal. "Call the expedition together and I'll let them know what's decided."

"Yes, Sir." She scampered off to find the other members of the team. The tea had nicely steeped when she returned with Pentam.

"Had to let him finish in the darkroom."

Sir Shillingsworth nodded.

"We'll be turning north to follow the edge of the mat. Captain Cully will try to stay close enough for us to see clearly, but far enough away to prevent the weed catching in the screw. We will keep watches on both port and starboard, but only a couple of people need watch the starboard. We'll trade off so everyone has a fair chance at boredom."

The scientists laughed and headed for the deck.

Cal still needed to ask about the size and shape of the screw. Though it drove the ship, she only had a foggy notion of what it might look like. The risk of it tangling suggested a slightly different shape than she'd imagined. She figured out the rudder by peering over the stern, until Sam asked her to stop as she was making him nervous.

"You slip, you'd get chewed up, and there'd be nothing left to rescue."

Cal added his warning to the picture in her mind.

The Peregrine steamed slowly north while they scanned the endless mat. Cal spotted a pod of whales on the starboard side and captured a quick sketch before they vanished as fast as they'd come.

The boat came and went to check the edge of the mat. The only difference from the smaller mats was the size of the weeds. They found much larger specimens in the immense mat. Each night at dusk, the Peregrine would pull away from the mat

and chug just enough to stay in position a safe distance from the seaweed.

To Pentam's dismay, Cal took the opportunity to visit the engine room and learn more about how Monky managed the changes in speed. But Dr. Franklyn commented that no knowledge was wasted, so she let the boy stew.

"Can't let the fire go down too far, or it's the devil to heat the boiler agin. Use the pressure valve to slow the steam through the cut-off to the pistons." He pointed to the valve in question. Cal recognized it from her training, but she'd never used it. "Tis a waste of coal, but it gives us headway. To start her up you need more pressure through t'cylinder. You need to wear them gloves." Monky pointed to the wall. "The steam makes everything mighty hot."

With her trips to the engine room, Cal's sleep pattern was thrown off again. She woke with the porthole still dark. Sleep refused to return, so she got dressed and, grabbing her satchel, headed up on deck.

"Hoy, Cal." Sam called to her from the top deck. "Come on up."

She climbed the ladder to the deck which ran around the top level of the Peregrine above the bridge.

"How was the night?"

"Quiet." Sam yawned. "No sea monsters, nothing but weeds and water."

Cal settled where she could watch the west side and still catch Sam at the rail scanning the water. The sun lifted above the horizon and light burst across the world illuminating the mat.

"Oh wow." Cal pointed to the west. "Take a look at that." She didn't wait for Sam's response but slid down the ladder and ran to Sir Shillingsworth's door.

"You'll want to see this, Sir." She shouted through the door. After a mumbled response, she ran back out onto the deck.

The feel of the engines shifted as the bridge brought the Peregrine closer to the mat. The others stumbled out onto the deck.

"What's got you so excited...?" Lahdin looked at Cal then west and froze.

Sir Shillingsworth and Pentam appeared on deck and joined the crowd at the rail.

No more than a quarter mile into the mat, ships floated in various degrees of disrepair. Much of their decks and even masts were covered with plant life. Even from this distance, Cal could see movement on the ships.

"Those have to be the biggest crabs I've ever seen." Lahdin pointed toward the ships. "The legs must be six feet across."

"Wonder how they'd taste?" Prof. Orthin licked his lips. "Do we have enough butter on board?" He laughed with the others.

"I'd expect them to be too tough and strong flavoured for eating, but you're welcome to try." Sir Shillingsworth pulled his spyglass from his coat and put it to his eye. "There's no shortage of specimens." He handed the glass to Lahdin. "I'll ask the Captain to hold us steady relative to the ships. Take what observations you can from the deck. I don't want to try going into the seaweed with the rowboat until we know a lot more about it."

When the spyglass made its way to Cal, she alternated between peering through it at the ships and sketching madly. Halfway through the morning she had to go to her equipment locker to get more sketchbooks. She was a long way from running out. Lots of bigger sheets too. Cal put the full books in and took out fresh ones. On impulse, she grabbed a couple of the largest sheets.

Sam and Henrichs found a folding table they set up on the deck. Cal spread out the paper and worked on a panorama of the weed, the ships and the crabs scuttling about, with birds soaring over it all.

***

Pentam set up his camera, but even in the dead calm the ship moved too much to get a photo. He put the equipment away before his frustration made him do something stupid.

Cal sat at a table drawing with her usual grace and speed. The camera couldn't compete with her. Pentam rubbed his stomach. Since she'd decided to ignore his advice and work in the engine room they'd hardly talked.

Nothing had happened to her, thank God, but she didn't seem to realize how dangerous it was. She certainly didn't care that he lay up nights worried about her, waiting for the screams which would tell him the engine room had claimed another victim. He couldn't understand how Sir Shillingsworth allowed it.

Fortunately, since they'd arrived in the Sargasso, Cal had been mostly on deck. He'd seen her sneak down to the engine room now and again, but he kept his peace. She'd made her feelings clear.

Without anything to do, Pentam wandered into the lab. The chemistry set-up mocked him. He didn't know how to use half the equipment. It would be the end of his career.

"Could you use a hand with the chemistry?" Pentam turned to see Matt standing at the door.

"You know chemistry?"

"It was my major until I switched to fish." Matt came in and looked at the chemistry lab. "I'm not sure about this." He pointed to a complex of beakers and coiled copper tubing. "Unless it's meant to concentrate the sample to make testing easier. These are reagents for testing for specific compounds." He went through the equipment identifying what he knew and shrugging over the mysteries. "Do I pass? You're the only one without an assistant and Prof Orthin gave me permission."

"I'll be honest with you." Pentam ran his hand along the table. *Gritty, I should clean it.* "I'm not supposed to be the chemist on the team. The man Sir Shillingsworth hired insulted Cal, then

115

demanded she be left on shore. I've worked for Sir Shillingsworth a few years now, and I've never seen him so angry. He didn't have time to hire another man, so he dumped it on me."

"Oh man. I wondered why you weren't fussing at it the way the others were at their equipment."

"Yeah, we might as well have no chemist at all. I don't have much more background than you." Pentam's hand clenched. He couldn't blame Sir Shillingsworth; he should have argued.

"How about we approach it as a team? If we run into something we don't know I'm sure the others would help."

"You think so? At the university, someone in my position would be eaten alive."

"We aren't at university; we're on a science vessel in the middle of the ocean. Besides what have we got to lose?"

Pentam grinned suddenly and put his hand out.

"Welcome to the chemistry department. Let's start with something simple. What about pH values?"

"Sounds good to me. We have enough samples of the seaweed to run tests. I can ask Dr. Franklyn what reagents might be worth trying too."

"You go do that, I'm going to get this cleaned up and ready for work."

Pentam worked all morning, and by the time he had everything sparkling and free of contaminants, Matt returned with a list of suggestions. He put it on a cork board beside the table.

"Let's get going."

Pentam stood and stretched after noting the pH of a green variety of seaweed. Like the others it was slightly more acidic than the water around them. If he'd been on the ball he'd have taken tests at each stop where they picked up the samples. He'd just have to acknowledge the gap and live with it.

"Good." Sir Shillingsworth walked into the lab. "I was hoping you'd get started."

"I'm sorry, Sir. I should have been on it long before."

"Pentam, I threw you into waters well out of your depth. Whatever you do will be more than we have now. Do what you can do, and do it well, and you'll be fine."

Working in the lab helped Pentam stop worrying about Cal and her stubborn determination to put herself at risk. There wasn't room in his head for chemistry and that infuriating girl.

***

Through the day, the scientists took samples from the mat, capturing a plethora of tiny creatures with the seaweed. Cal remembered the lens Pentam had given her and used it to see detail on the smaller animals. Using it twisted her heart strangely, but she put the feeling aside and focused on work. She had no time to waste trying to understand Pentam.

As the sun lowered toward the horizon, Prof Orthin announced he wanted to check the depth of the seaweed. Sam volunteered to row the boat. Cal couldn't sketch in the dim light, and besides was the only one not busy since Matt had disappeared into the lab.

They launched the boat and Sam rowed steadily toward the mat of seaweed. Prof Orthin pulled out a rope with knots at regular intervals. He had a tube with glass at one end he used to look under water.

They rowed to within a dozen feet of the mat.

"This will do." Prof Orthin pulled a glass ball from his bag and shook it hard. It started glowing brightly in his hands. "A friend of mine developed it for me, developed the reaction from studying algae and fungi." He tied the rope to the loop at the top of the ball.

Cal peered over the side, but the water swallowed all light.

"I needed to wait for evening when the sunlight wouldn't interfere with the light from the ball." He put the ball in the water then handed the rope to Sam. "Lower the ball slowly. Count out as each knot enters the water."

"Like sounding for depth," Sam said.

"Exactly so." The Professor put his tube in the water. "Please start." He peered down into the depths of the ocean.

"One...two...three...."

The numbers grew slowly and steadily. Cal pulled out her sketchbook, and as much by touch as sight sketched the scene of Sam lowering the ball, leaning over the water, with Prof. Orthin also leaning over looking through his tube. The Peregrine in the background had her running lights on, and figures lined the rail watching them.

They pulled up the ball, moved over a hundred yards and sent the ball down again. The next time Sam pulled up the ball he handed Cal his knife.

"Some cheese in the bag, cut a few slices for us."

When she'd finished, Sam was leaning over counting knots, so she folded the knife and put it under the seat.

"Hold up." Prof. Orthin sat up and stretched. He motioned to Cal. "Want to have a look?"

She put down her sketchbook to switch places with Prof. Orthin. Far down in the depths, the ball shone as a pinprick of light. By the faint glow she could see the where the weed stopped. Cal lifted her eye.

"How deep is the ball?"

"Sixty feet, much further than I expected."

Cal returned to the tube.

"The light is gone."

"Strange." Prof. Orthin switched back to his seat and peered down. "The chemical reaction should have lasted longer. Perhaps the pressure or the cold has affected it." He waved at Sam. "You may as well pull it up."

Sam began pulling the rope, letting it coil on the bottom of the boat.

"It's stuck." Perhaps it's caught on a bit of seaweed, give it a good tug."

Sam stood and gave a great heave on the rope, it came up a little, then something yanked it out of his hands. He staggered back as the rope roared over the gunwale of the boat, tilting it toward the water. The rope tangled around his foot which had landed on it when he stumbled.

"My knife!" Sam scrabbled at the rope. Cal dove for the knife and came up with it in her hand, flipping it open as she stretched to hand it to Sam.

The rope around his leg snapped taut and dragged him overboard. He grabbed at the gunwale tilting the boat more. Cal lost her balance and fell to the bottom of the boat. Her head hit something, making the world spin. The boat rocked violently again. She reached for the end of the rope, but it flipped over the side and vanished. Her head hurt. Prof. Orthin took the knife from her, folded it and put it on the seat. Then he helped Cal to sit up.

"Are you all right?" Cal nodded but that set the world to spinning again. She closed her eyes for a moment and leaned forward. When she opened her eyes, she saw the sketch of Sam. Water had splashed on it as if it wanted to claim even this drawing of the man. She looked over the side, hoping to see him come to the surface, but nothing disturbed the black surface of the water.

He was gone.

Cal's heart wrenched and tears flowed from her eyes. She ruthlessly pushed away the sobs which threatened to incapacitate her.

"We'd better get back to the ship." Cal winced at the cold, even words coming from her mouth. Prof. Orthin nodded and they clumsily took the oars and rowed back toward the Peregrine. The oars blistered her hands within minutes. She welcomed the pain as a distraction from the greater pain within her. If she'd been faster, if she hadn't borrowed the knife. If she hadn't been focused on drawing pictures.

Why had she come? Her heart ached the way it had when her mother succumbed to fever, leaving Cal alone overnight. Alive and talking in the evening, cold and stiff when Cal went to wake her in the morning. Cal didn't know how long she tried to wake her mother before a servant found Cal and carried her screaming out of the room. Even after all these years, the memory reduced Cal to sobs. She didn't know if she wept for her mother, or Sam, or her own broken heart.

The boat bumped into the Peregrine. The crew caught the ropes and winched them up to where her father could lift her out of the boat and hold her tight while her tears soaked through his shirt and sobs wracked her body.

***

Cal woke in her berth, head wrapped in soft cloth. The gentlest of swells rocked her as light poured in the porthole. For the first time she could remember, her fingers didn't itch to draw something. Sam's death had done something to her. It was worse than that engineer's death. She'd eaten with Sam, played cards. He alone of the crew had always called her Cal.

They were friends.

Something unseen had taken him away, perhaps the thing they'd come to find. Despite the sailors' reservations, she'd been naïve. Cal hadn't thought of the expedition as dangerous. The eagerness for knowledge took on a different shape.

Was what they were doing worth the death of a friend? His knife lay in her bag. None of the crew wanted it. No one but Cal thought she might have prevented the tragedy.

"We're at sea, these things happen." Captain Cully said when she'd tried to apologize. It didn't help the guilt and grief eating at her heart. The *if only's* ate at her soul, the way they had with her mother. Even now, Cal wondered if she'd just stayed with her mother through the night. If only she were faster, smarter, more capable.

Cal stared at the ceiling of her berth and fought the tears leaking out of her eyes. Sobs shook her again and she curled up to give herself over to them. Through the day she cried until she felt hollow.

She wanted to go home. If she could have hitched a ride on an albatross she would have.

Chapter 10 Staying the Course

The conversation with her father came back to her. *There will be a time...* It had sounded so easy at home. What had he said at the end? *Stay the course.*

Would Father continue his work if it had been me? Cal sat up in her bunk. He would; she'd want him to. Grief was all very well, but moping in her berth was no fit memorial for Sam.

Cal got up and dressed with extra care. She replaced the water damaged sketchbook, but left the knife in the satchel. Time to get to work.

The deck hummed with activity. Captain Cully had determined the water was safe enough for the boats, but no more sounding ropes. They filled sample jars with fish, crabs and other things Cal couldn't identify. Shells and bones were cleaned and packed away, skins dried before they too were stowed below deck. Cal found a place out of the way and began recording the activity in her sketchbook.

Each of the scientists found an excuse to wander past and offer words of comfort and encouragement. Sir Shillingsworth caught her eye and nodded once. Pentam refused to look at her. She wasn't sure what had happened with him. They'd almost been friends when they'd left Finches Harbour.

The activity continued through the next days. The boats darted back and forth between the Peregrine and the weeds. A sailor waved with flags from the top deck. The boats adjusted their positions. One moved south to where birds flocked, pecking at the weed mat and pulling up crabs. They couldn't get close without entering the weeds. After a short time, the boat turned and returned to the Peregrine.

Cal cornered a crew member and had him teach her semaphore. She drew each letter out in her sketchbook.

The mess buzzed with conversation as the scientists talked and argued about their discoveries. They'd found scores of new creatures; others were known, but grew differently out here on the Sargasso weed. Strange fish which looked like floating clumps of seaweed, but feasted on shrimp and tiny crabs. Some of the crabs had long legs to spread their weight and allow them to scamper across the seaweed. Prof. Orthin had seen sharks

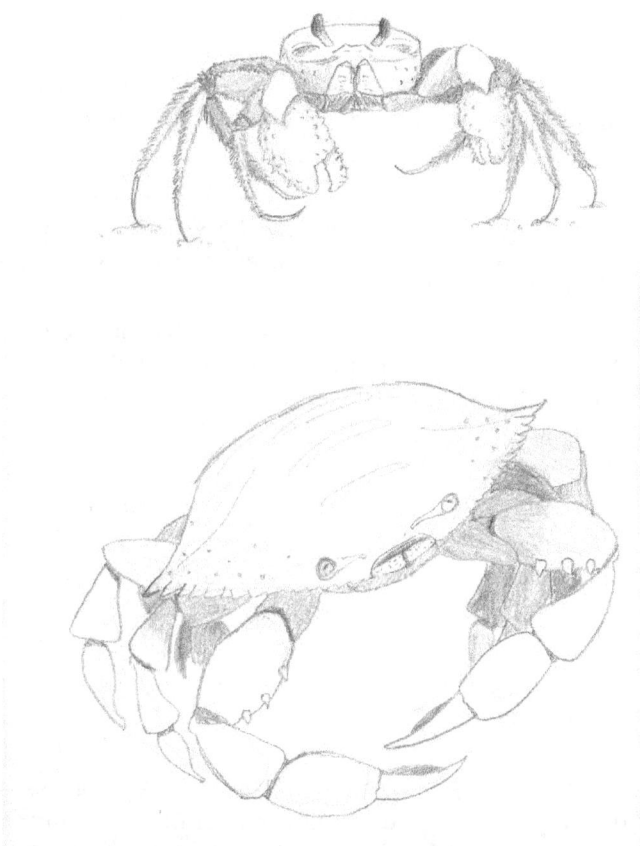

cruising along the edge of the mat, but hadn't managed to catch one yet. They were relatively small, he'd said, only eight or ten feet in length. Not big enough to pull a man out of a boat.

Cal forced her mind away from thinking of Sam.

"I'd like to get to those ships and study the big crabs." Lahdin said between bites.

"Captain Cully will allow one boat to enter the seaweed tomorrow." Sir Shillingsworth set his cutlery down. "Not far at first. Slow is best."

"Why is it the Captain's decision?" Dan scraped at his plate.

"They're his boats, and he is responsible for the safety of us and the crew." Sir Shillingsworth spoke casually, but Dan nodded, then went back to the galley to get another plate of food.

***

In the morning, the scientists drew straws for the privilege of entering the seaweed. Prof Orthin and Dan won. Captain Cully assigned two sailors to row the largest of the three boats.

"Your job until they return is to keep watch." Sir Shillingsworth handed Cal his spyglass. "Alert them of any danger."

"Yes, Sir." Cal stowed her drawing materials and took the glass, following the boat's progress to the weeds. The Peregrine held station a hundred yards from the edge of the mat. The flurry of study determined that was a safe compromise between convenience for study and clearance from the seaweed.

The boat hardly slowed when it first entered the mat. It looked solid from the ship, but like a marsh, it deluded the unwary. The scientists moved carefully to the sides of the boat, and nets in hand scooped up creatures, peered at them, then put them back or put them in a sample jar for later study.

Throughout the morning, they zigzagged perhaps a hundred yards into the weed, their progress slowed as they went deeper. From the waving arms, Cal could tell the scientists were arguing with the sailors. They went no deeper; instead they headed toward the spot where the birds chose to fight over whatever crab or fish they caught.

Something moved on the edge of the spyglass' circle. She swung the glass. Hadn't there been a bird there a second ago? Keeping the boat on the periphery of the circle, Cal watched the birds. She could see gulls, pelicans, and others she couldn't name. They flew down, snatched a meal, then flapped up to hover awkwardly to eat.

Why waste the energy? She'd seen any number of birds floating on the surface around the Peregrine.

A gull missed its prey and took time to try again. A snakelike head popped out of the weed-filled water and caught the bird as easily as the gull had caught the smaller creatures. Cal gasped and sat back, almost dropping the glass.

"Sir Shillingsworth!" she shouted, then put her eye to the glass. Nobody in the boat reacted to the creature's appearance. They didn't know the danger they were in.

"What, Cal?" Sir Shillingsworth's shadow fell across her.

"Something is eating the birds, big enough to pull them under easily." She handed him the glass and pointed. "Watch for one to stay too long near the water." Cal stood up and screened her eyes with her hand. She couldn't see much beyond moving specks of white.

She felt more than saw Sir Shillingsworth stiffen.

"Good work." He handed the glass back to Cal and walked over to a sailor. After a couple of words, the man ran up to the bridge. A moment later the boom of the ship's horn made Cal start and clutch the spyglass. She put it to her eye.

The crew on the boat were pointing to the ship, while the scientists stowed their gear. Prof. Orthin pointed at the flock; Dan looked but shook his head. The sailors were already rowing the boat quickly back toward the Peregrine. The other boats arrived and were winched into place and disgorged their passengers onto the deck. When the third boat arrived, Prof. Orthin climbed over the side then went to the rail beside Sir Shillingsworth and scanned the weeds.

"I take it you called us back because of whatever was eating the birds?"

"Yes, we need to plan carefully how we are going to capture one of them. Cal spotted them first."

The professor came over to her.

"Well done." He sat, then stood again. "Sorry, but sitting in that boat has made me crave standing. Would you be able to sketch what you saw?"

Cal handed him the spyglass and pulled out her materials. Drawing from memory was tricky, details shifted in her mind, and she'd only had the briefest glimpse. She closed her eyes and sketched the picture on the back of her eyelids. The gull diving down, staying a little too long. The black head erupting from under weeds to snatch it.

Her fingers flew across the paper. She hardly looked at what she drew. A collective gasp brought her awareness back from wherever it had been. A crowd hovered around her, peering at the drawing.

"That's no fish."

"Don't know what it is; never seen the like."

"Looks like something my gramps told me about when I was a kid. He'd seen it on his last voyage."

"What was that?"

"A sea serpent, though from Gramps' telling it was some bigger than that." A sailor named Thomas spoke up.

Some laughed while others nodded their heads.

"Sea serpents aren't real, are they?" Hank asked, looking at Prof. Orthin.

"Real enough my gramps never went back to sea," Thomas said.

Cal studied the drawing. The creature's snout looked too long for a snake, more like a crocodile. She'd never seen teeth like that on any snake her father had shown her.

"So now what?" Cal looked up at Sir Shillingsworth.

"We plan how we are going to capture one of those things."

The crowd stirred, then broke into groups, the crew returning to their duties, the scientists to plotting traps.

Cal didn't think she was supposed to hear her father murmur.

"I wonder just how big they grow."

Chapter 11 Capturing a Myth

"We need a net." Pentam leaned against the wall of the lab. "Remember catching that ostrich, Sir Shillingsworth?" He desperately wanted to be in on the capture. Chemistry was important, but boring. This was where the excitement was.

"A net, yes, but the seaweed is a problem. We can't sink it below the surface." Prof. Orthin scratched his head.

"So we bait the creature up onto the net." Pentam waved his hands in illustration. "Then haul it up."

"We don't know how long this thing is." Lahdin looked up from where he doodled on scrap of paper.

"The snout looks like a crocodile to me," Cal spoke up. "How long would a crocodile be?"

"Eight feet? Maybe ten? Hard to say without a good sense of scale." Sir Shillingsworth peered at the drawing.

"So we need to get the thing eight feet onto the net?" Pentam paced the room in frustration.

"And how are you going to keep it there?" Cal asked.

"I don't know, shoot it? Spear it?" Pentam bit back the snarl. She almost died, again, and here she was angling to put herself at risk again. "All we need is a few seconds when it's tangled...." An idea flitted at the edges of his mind. "Cal, may I borrow your sketchbook?" The others stirred, but Cal handed him the book and pencil without question. He looked in her eyes and saw no anger. *I don't have time for this.*

Pentam scribbled in the book scratching out an idea, then crossing it off, and trying another. The lab stayed quiet as he worked. Cal made no protest when he flipped the page and kept scribbling. Then another. *Got it. It will work.* He looked at his drawing and gave a choked laugh. He went to tear the pages out.

"Please don't." Cal held her hand out.

Pentam put the book in her hand and scrubbed at his eyes. He could see it so clearly, why did it come out as a mess?

"We need to flip the net. Use the finest we think will hold the beast. Use ropes to turn it over and tangle the creature. It looks like it has a spine ridge, that will hook the webbing and hold it." The others were looking at each other trying to imagine the picture from his words.

"Like this?" Cal held her book out to him. He looked at the page and saw his plan pictured perfectly in a series of drawings.

"This is amazing. I could kiss you." Pentam held the book up to show the others.

"Maybe later." Cal's words sent his heart flipping and his words dried up.

"It will work." Prof. Orthin took the book from Pentam's nerveless fingers and examined it. "We have everything we need. It will take two boats."

Pentam stopped hearing them as they huddled around the drawing.

Sir Shillingsworth slapped him on the shoulder.

"Well done."

Pentam shook himself and joined the scrum around the drawing.

When they'd decided everything down to the weight of the net and how to get the ropes in position, to what size bird they needed for bait and if it should be alive or dead. Pentam stretched and excused himself. The others grinned at him and went back to arguing details.

Pentam walked out onto the deck. The moon had risen; it illuminated Cal standing at the bow of the Peregrine. Her shoulders were shaking as she stared over the side. Pentam's heart thumped painfully and his palms were wet. He forced his feet to carry him over to her side.

Cal looked at him, the moonlight making the tears on her cheeks glisten silver.

God, she's so beautiful. He reached out to hold her shoulder then let his hand fall. She was so much more than he deserved.

Cal threw herself into his arms. Pentam stopped thinking, holding her tight as weeping shook her. Time stopped there in the moonlight, her warm body against his. She said something into his shoulder, and he loosened his grip so he could see her and hear her voice.

"Oh Pentam."

"I'm sorry about Sam." Pentam brushed his hand across her hair, soft as silk on his fingers.

Cal shook her head.

"We were friends, you and I," she whispered and looked up again, her face silver and black. "What did I do? Why have you stopped caring?"

Her words hit him like a shot to the heart. He thought he could die on the spot. His voice deserted him, left him gasping for air. Without him thinking about it, he tilted his head down just a little and kissed her on the lips.

She tasted of salt, of something incredibly sweet. Her arms wrapped tighter around him and she kissed him back. Time stopped again. Pain, uncertainty, fear, anger all fled his heart as it filled with something else.

Aeons later, they let go of each other and stepped back. Cal dropped her head. Pentam lifted it with a finger.

"I never stopped caring." Pentam whispered. "I didn't know how to watch you in danger. I'm a coward when it comes to you."

"I can't stop," Cal said.

"I know, I'll learn how to live with it."

"Did my drawing help?"

"You were there, weren't you? It was brilliant; like you'd drawn what was in my head."

"I left right after I gave the book to you. I didn't want to break down in front of everyone."

"And I stayed and didn't even notice." Pentam's throat clogged.

Cal put her finger on his lips. "You came. It doesn't matter how long it took. You came." She stood on her toes and kissed him gently. "Goodnight, Pentam."

Cal left him alone on the deck. He stared out over the ocean, white and black.

Sir Shillingsworth joined him at the rail. They stood in silent companionship. In every one of their expeditions, there was a moment when all the world stilled and Pentam marvelled at how he was part of it.

"Be careful with Cal's heart, Son."

A chill ran down Pentam's spine.

"You saw?"

"We're on a ship." Sir Shillingsworth's lips bent into a faint smile. He wrapped his arm around Pentam's shoulder. "She's got good taste." He shook Pentam gently then wandered off leaving Pentam staring at the ocean without seeing a thing.

***

Cal woke with a smile and took a moment to lie in the sunlight and recall every moment of that kiss. She'd walked past her father and given him a look. He'd smiled back at her, though he looked a little sad.

She refrained from entering details of the kiss in the expedition's log. Instead she wrote in one of her sketchbooks, drawing a picture of Pentam's face in the moonlight. She couldn't get the eyes right. Cal doubted paper and pencil could capture that glow.

Time to get to work. Cal got up and dressed, checked her satchel, then headed for breakfast. She resisted the temptation to sit beside Pentam, deep in discussion with Henrichs. Her father waved her over.

"You all right?" He stared into his tea.

"More than all right." Cal couldn't keep the grin from her face.

"He's a good man." Sir Shillingsworth wrapped his arm around her and squeezed. "Be careful, hearts are fragile things."

Cal leaned her head on his shoulder for a bit, relishing the contact with her father. He'd never been one for hugs.

After breakfast Cal rescued her sketchbook from the lab, using a large piece of paper to copy the drawing. She wasn't going to risk losing Pentam's drawings. He'd be furious, but they were precious, the moment when they began to reconnect.

The rest of the day she spent sketching as Pentam directed the team in putting the equipment together. He found her larger drawing and walked around comparing it with the growing pile on the deck. At one point, he saw her sketching him and blew her a kiss.

She captured it then stared at it a while, letting the warm feelings run through her.

At supper Pentam sat beside her and gave her hand a squeeze. Prof Orthin winked at her and she blushed, but she didn't let go of Pentam's hand.

That evening, all the preparations were done, and it was a matter of waiting for daylight. The team sat in the mess telling stories while Pentam held Cal's hand. Everyone knew, and it didn't bother them. Cal sighed and smiled up at Pentam, transfixed by Dr. Franklyn's tale of finding a never-before-seen orchid in the jungle.

As they started wandering off to bed, Cal dragged Pentam out to the bow. They stood watching nothing for a while.

"You'd better get some sleep if you're leading this thing tomorrow." Cal sighed. "I wish I could stand here all night with you."

"Your father might have something to say about that."

"Father knows." Cal wrapped her arms around Pentam's arm and hugged it tight. "He just wants us to be careful."

"I would never hurt you." Pentam turned and lifted her chin.

"People hurt each other all the time." Cal smiled at him. "Mother and Father sometimes got into awful fights, but they always made up." She stood on her toes and kissed him. His arms wrapped tightly around her and in that moment, she'd never felt safer.

"Be careful tomorrow." Cal brushed her hand across his cheek. "I won't say it as you get in the boat, so I'm saying it now."

"Nothing's going to keep me away from you." Pentam leaned down and brushed his lips against hers. Cal shivered and watched him walk through the door to the men's berths.

"You can come out now, Father."

Sir Shillingsworth stepped out of the shadow and walked over to her.

"It's good to see you happy."

Cal hugged him.

"You never hugged me much before. It was like it pained you to be touched."

"In some ways it did. I miss your mother so much sometimes it's like she only died yesterday. I let that get in the way of being a good father for you." Her father held her close.

"You've always been a good father. You've been fair, you listened to me, you let me run around in dresses covered with pockets and charcoal on fingers. I must have been a terrible embarrassment to you."

"I've always been proud of you, and never more so than on this trip."

Cal gave her father one last hug and headed to bed.

***

Cal's fingers were busy capturing the scene on the deck. Henrichs stood on the deck with a harpoon in one hand. She'd dressed in plain whites.

"Spent some time spear fishing here and there. Thought I'd bring her for backup."

"You sure you want to command the boat?" Sir Shillingsworth came up beside her.

"Wouldn't send a man out if I weren't willing to go myself."

Sir Shillingsworth nodded and stepped up to talk to the six who were set to hunt the sea serpent.

"I'd like to come along myself, but each of you has been chosen for your skills. Be careful. I'd rather lose a specimen than any one of you. Now, Pentam go through the plan one more time."

141

Pentam looked at Sir Shillingsworth in shock and Cal giggled.

"Your plan, your command." Sir Shillingsworth said with a smile.

"All right...." Pentam got over his nerves as he got into the plan they'd developed from his initial idea. As he finished, the seagull a sailor had snared the day before squawked loudly. Pentam laughed. "See, he knows his part."

The men climbed into the smaller boat and were launched. As Pentam waited with Henrichs and Dr. Franklyn, Cal slipped up and gave Pentam a kiss.

"For good luck. I'll be watching."

"Come on, you lucky guy, it's our turn." Henrichs punched his arm lightly. Pentam blushed and climbed into the boat. Henrichs winked at Cal and climbed after him. Dr. Franklyn handed in the box with the sea gull then boarded the boat.

The team members who weren't in the boats lined the railing. Sir Shillingsworth had his spyglass to his eye, so Cal stood at the rail with the others and peered.

"Heh, Missy." Monky came up beside her. "Heard ye'was hunting sea serpents."

"That's what the crew's calling them." Cal didn't take her eyes off the boats.

"This young man of yours, is he a good'un?"

"One of the best."

"No less than you deserve, Missy." Monky slid something into her hand. "Happens I won a spyglass in a card game. Don't have much use fer it in the engine room. And if my beau was out after sea serpents, I'd want t'see clear. Draw me a pict're when th're done." He vanished as quickly as he'd come.

Cal extended the glass and watched through it.

The boats neared the weed, heading to where the birds flocked today. A different location than the days before. *To find fresh prey, or to stay ahead of the serpents?* Closer to the feeding birds they passed the net between the boats and unrolled it carefully. Ropes on each side ran over to the opposite boat. They kept rowing closer to the flock, and stopped when the birds started to look nervous.

Then the waiting started. Gradually during the course of the morning, the flock shifted closer to the boats. The people in the boats might have been statues.

"That should do it." Sir Shillingsworth muttered.

As if they'd heard him, Dr. Franklyn reached into the box and pulled out the gull. It flapped wildly sending feathers everywhere. He tossed it into the net. A weight on its leg kept it from escaping.

Wings flapped at the water, then slowed as the bird exhausted itself. Cal had about given up on getting a reaction, when the water beneath the bait heaved up. A head with pointed jaws pushed through the net to clamp down on the gull. The men in the boats hauled on the ropes, hoping to flip the net and catch their prey before it could escape.

The creature thrashed in the water, almost pulling the ropes free. The boats rocked and Dr. Franklyn came close to falling overboard. Then the serpent rolled toward Pentam's boat snapping at the ropes. Cal's heart skipped a beat as she imagined the thing in the boat biting and slashing at Pentam.

Henrich's harpoon flashed, striking the serpent behind the head. It stiffened then went limp. They might have lost it still, but for the rope on the harpoon.

They dragged the net to the larger boat, and with the help of the harpoon pulled the beast into the craft. Cal estimated it at ten feet in length by the time it lay in the bottom. They rowed back to the cheers of the men at the rail.

Cal collapsed the spyglass and drew the approach of the triumphant hunters.

The boats were winched up, and the gear unloaded. Last they lifted the sea serpent onto the deck. Pentam strode over to Cal and gave her a strong kiss. The people around cheered. Cal blushed, then grabbed his hair to kiss him harder.

***

The rest of the morning, Pentam recorded the serpent in detail with his camera, while Cal watched with a smile on her lips, letting her fingers dance across the pages drawing him and the fascinated crew and scientists. When Prof. Orthin and Lahdin dragged it to the lab for dissection, Pentam followed with his camera, and Cal with her sketchbook.

This was the reason for the long table. Even so the tail hung off the end. It looked like nothing Cal had ever seen, and she'd been recording her father's finds for years. Dan and Matt held the thing still while Prof. Orthin cut into it.

The creature stank worse than any fish. Its stench made Cal's eyes burn. Dr. Franklyn opened a cupboard while the professor gagged and coughed. She left, while the doctor passed out masks and goggles to the four men working on the dissection. He followed out her out onto the deck.

Professor Orthin made a report at supper. "It isn't a snake, and it isn't a fish. The thing has rudimentary legs which work as fins, and lungs to breathe air. The skin is leathery like a crocodile."

"We've agreed on a name, though we don't have a proper taxonomy yet." Lahdin grinned as if that were a great joke. "The scientific name for the beast is *serpens marinus calliope.*

145

Cal's face burned as the others cheered.

"You were the first to spot it." The Professor pointed to her. "The honour is yours."

"I'm not sure how to thank you for naming something with such a large mouth and so many teeth after me." Cal took a large bite from the bun in her hand and mess cheered again.

"Congratulations." Sir Shillingsworth joined her on the deck to watch the sun go down. "I believe it was my third or fourth expedition before something was named after me. A rather unique mouse, more ears than body."

Cal leaned against him.

"Thanks for the advice, Father."

"Advice?"

"Stay the course. I almost gave up after Sam died. Then I wondered what you would have done if it had been me. I'd want you to keep going. So I got out of bed and...." She waved her hand. "I have a man who I think I love, a great ugly serpent with my name. What more could a woman want?"

Sir Shillingsworth laughed and kissed the top of Cal's head.

"We all take risks; every time we climb out of bed we head into danger. Out here it's a little closer." He patted her hand on the rail. "I'll leave you now so your man can spend some time with you."

Chapter 12   The Maw of the Serpent

Pentam lay on his bunk and grinned. Cal had left him with a kiss which set his whole body to tingling. His plan to capture the serpent had worked to perfection. It didn't even bother him that Cal got the honour of it being named after her. She deserved it. He'd have plenty of opportunity.

Pentam organized a couple more excursions to capture the sea serpents. They caught two over the course of the week. A small one, under eight feet in length went into one of the immense preserving jars. The larger one, over fifteen feet, was dissected, its bones and skin cleaned, dried and packed away with the first.

Dan suggested testing to find what the chemical was which made eyes burn during dissection. They discovered it was a very concentrated hydrofluoric acid.

Alex McGilvery

"Perhaps it helps the serpent digest its meals. The dissection showed it doesn't use those teeth to chew."

"That would make sense." Pentam capped the sample then slid the goggles up his face. "It would be easier to wear these in a cooler climate." He used a handkerchief to wipe his face.

"We have three specimens; how many does Sir Shillingsworth want to take?"

"I think a couple more. Another small one, and he seems to think they get much bigger, he's cooking up a way to catch a big one. Our method almost didn't work on that fifteen-footer.

"What's he thinking?" Dan cleaned up the chemistry table, being careful not to splash any liquid on his skin.

"He was muttering about a harpoon gun like whalers use."

"That'd be great if we had one." Dan put the rag in the garbage and led the way out of the lab. "You go spend some time with Cal."

***

The two boats floated on the seaweed. They were confident enough in their method that Cal tagged along on the larger boat, sketchbook in hand. They'd reached the point where complete stillness was needed. Even Cal's pencil had stilled. Pentam released the bait into the net. She had a horrific vision of a monster leaping up and swallowing him. Shaking her head, she focused on the net. The flapping of the bird set her heart thumping in the same rhythm as if it were there on the net. The nearby flock circled and flew away.

"Something's wrong," Pentam called. "Be sharp. If the thing is too big, let go of the rope. I won't risk people for a specimen."

A vision of Sam vanishing into the depths invaded her mind making her fingers shake too much to draw. As Cal put the sketchbook in her satchel her fingers brushed against the knife.

"Pentam, tell people to be sure they're clear of the ropes."

She hadn't finished speaking when a huge wave heaved out of the water. Cal caught the briefest glimpse of immense teeth before net and bird vanished under the water. Pentam had turned to look at her when she spoke. The rope wrapped around his leg and pulled him over the side.

Cal screamed and dove forward over the side. Rope burned past her. Putting the knife in her teeth, she gripped the rope and pulled herself down as seaweed slashed at her face. Hand over hand she got closer to Pentam. He looked up at her with horror on his face. Cal pulled harder, faster. Pentam reached up and took the knife from her mouth and with one slash cut the rope. He clutched the knife in one hand looking around for danger, then grabbing Cal's hand, he kicked for the surface. Her body bucked with the need to breath. Cal grabbed Pentam's face and kissed him, forcing his

149

mouth open with her tongue, then breathing into him while he breathed back. They kicked for the surface again, fighting the seaweed.

They weren't going to make it. They'd die here. Her mind calculated exactly how much time they had left. Cal looked at Pentam. She could do worse than die with him.

Then Thomas plunged down through the weeds with a rope around his waist. He gripped Pentam and Cal around the waist, then kicked the rope hard three times. They soared up through the water, past the weeds to break the surface.

Cal's gasp for air sounded more like a scream. She looked for Pentam and saw him holding the side of the boat, panting for air. The sailor hoisted Cal and tossed her into the boat before climbing in himself. Cal crawled over to Pentam and clutched at him, her hand running over him to make sure he was all there.

"Sorry, Cal." Pentam coughed and spat out water. "I dropped your knife."

"I'd rather have you than a knife." Cal put her head on his chest and closed her eyes. They were safe.

Henrichs wrapped a blanket around them before they rowed at speed back to the boat. Her father lifted her out of the boat and crushed her to him. To Cal's horror, tears ran down his face. When Pentam staggered onto the deck, Sir

Shillingsworth reached out and pulled him into a hug.

"I thought I'd lost you, both of you." His voice shook. He finally let them go and dashed at the tears on his face. Sir Shillingsworth opened his mouth to say something, but turned and abruptly walked away.

"What happened to your face?" Pentam looked at her with wide eyes.

Cal rubbed her fingers across her cheek and felt a sting, she looked at her fingers, and they were red with blood.

"Purser!" Pentam shouted. "Someone get the Purser."

"It's just a scratch, Silly." Cal shook her head. The world spun and went black.

**

Pentam watched Cal slump on the deck and his heart almost stopped.

"She's still breathing." Henrichs crouched down beside him. "While the purser is caring for Cal, I want to look at that leg of yours.

Pentam looked down and saw his ankle raw and oozing blood. He winced as the pain hit him. Someone passed him a glass of brandy. He drank it down as Henrichs splashed more on his ankle. She wrapped it in white cloth until he couldn't see the blood seep through.

Alex McGilvery

"Watch it carefully, keep it wrapped up unless the Purser or I am checking it. With the seawater, you should be good."

Pentam looked over and Cal had gone, leaving a smear of blood on the deck.

"She's just in shock. The Purser will treat her cuts and keep her warm. He'll let you know when you can visit. "I'm going to check on Sir Shillingsworth." Henrichs walked away, while Dan and Matt hauled him up and carried him to the mess.

"You won't want to sleep before you see Cal."

"I've never seen anything like it." Dan shivered. "She hit the water only a few seconds after you. The rope ran so fast it burned a gouge in the gunwale of the boat. When neither of you came up, Thomas wrapped another rope around him and dove in after you. Henrichs was yelling something about throwing him in the brig. He came up dragging both of you, and my heart about burst. I'd much rather attend your wedding than your funeral."

The brandy had hit Pentam's system and he let the word *wedding* float about in his consciousness. He'd wait until they were on shore and he could get a proper ring.

Dan shook him awake.

"Cal's ready to see you."

152

Pentam limped with Dan's help to the infirmary, next to the Purser's office.

"She's resting, but she wanted to see you before she slept." The Purser put a hand on Pentam's shoulder. "The whole time I was stitching her up, she was asking after you."

Pentam pushed through the door into the room where Cal lay, almost as white as the sheets. She smiled brightly at him when he entered, then winced.

"It will be a while before I can smile. I'll need to practice being as serious as Father."

"I've never seen him like he is on this trip."

"Me neither, I like it." Cal reached out and Pentam took her hand. He watched as her eyes fluttered closed. For a long time, he sat listening to her breathe. When exhaustion threatened to make him fall over, he brushed his lips over hers. Her lips twitched and she sighed.

***

Cal woke in a strange bed. Pain made her gasp when she sat up. The Purser stuck his head in the door.

"How are you feeling?"

She took inventory. Her face burned, and her hand ached.

"I'll live." Cal looked about. "I'd like to get dressed."

"No reason why not, I'll ask Henrichs to come and help. That hand will slow you down for a few days."

True to his word, Henrichs showed up with a dress over his arm. With a few twinges and a little awkwardness Cal exchanged her wrinkled underdress for fresh, then put her work dress over top. She wrinkled her nose at the blood on her underdress.

"We'll get it clean for you. Unfortunately, we have lots of experience cleaning blood out of whites."

Henrichs helped her stand and when her legs didn't fold Cal headed down to the mess.

The men rose when she entered and watched until she'd settled at a table. Pentam hobbled in a few minutes later and sat beside her.

"I guess it will be a while before you're drawing with that hand." He rubbed his finger feather-light across the bandage.

"I can draw left handed." Cal looked at her bandaged hand. "In a day or so it will be fine. I had worse scrapes as a kid."

"Why does that not surprise me?" Pentam leaned over and kissed her gently. "I couldn't believe when I looked up and you were coming down that rope with a knife in your mouth. You could have been a pirate."

"I didn't think. I had the knife open in my hand when you went over. It made sense to hold in my mouth and use my hands to get to you."

"You almost died." Pentam squeezed her left hand.

"So did you. When we were running out of air, I thought there would be worse things than dying with the man I loved." Heat ran through Cal's face, but she didn't turn her eyes away.

"I would hate to be the one to take you from this world."

Sir Shillingsworth walked into the mess.

"I've been talking with Captain Cully, and we've agreed we have all the samples we need." He held up his hand. "I know some of you wanted to get to the derelict ships, but this beast is an unknown and we have nothing on board to kill it." He looked around for argument, but no one spoke up. "Very well. Pack up your equipment. Finish with any samples you have. I want to be underway by dawn tomorrow." He spun and walked out.

"I think he's wise." Pentam said. "We can always return with a larger ship, maybe a whaler to take on the big one."

Cal's heart warmed when Pentam said *we.*

Stowing her drawing supplies was a simple matter of putting full books from her satchel into her locker.

Matt had insisted on packing the chemistry set-up, so Pentam was busy making his darkroom ready for travel.

Cal climbed up to the upper deck. Captain Cully waved at her as she passed. She took it as permission. A box made a good seat. She pulled out her sketchbook and took a pencil in her left hand. Despite her boast to Pentam, she hadn't seriously drawn with her left hand in years. The first couple of drawings were shaky, but by the time she'd been through several pages, her drawings were only imperceptibly different from her regular efforts.

Pentam walked out onto the stern deck where Thomas tidied the ropes preparing for the voyage home.

"The cook wanted me to catch a few fish for supper. It will be the last chance for a while unless they jump onto the ship on their own."

"Did you check with the Captain?" Thomas looked up for a moment.

"Henrichs said it should be OK. We haven't seen any of the serpents this far out. If something grabs the line, I'll let it go."

Cal set up to draw Pentam fishing. He tossed the line out gracefully and let it sink before hauling it up and doing again. On the third cast he caught a fish. He snapped its neck and kept on fishing. By the time the sun had moved to the west, he had a pile of fish on the deck.

On this cast, he must have hooked onto a larger fish. Pentam grunted as he hauled it in. It broke the surface and flapped desperately. Thomas run over with a long boathook and leaned over. Cal stood to get a better angle on their struggle. That was going to be a huge catch.

A shadow moved under the water. Shark, they'd seen a few, but nothing that big. It kept growing. Cal had a flash of the teeth pulling the net down.

"Pentam!" Cal screamed. "Get away from there, now." She pointed to the water. Pentam took one glance than dragged Thomas away from the side.

The serpent's head rose out of the water, catching the fish and still rising. It looked big enough to swallow a man. Pentam and Thomas scrambled back. The serpent turned to them and opened its mouth. It hit the Peregrine. The entire ship rocked violently and the serpent fell back into the water with a tremendous splash. Cal held on for dear life as the shadow vanished into the depths and the ship bobbed to a rest.

The *all hands* alarm sounded. Cal scrambled to pick up the sketchbook and stuff it in her satchel. The pencil was gone. She headed down the ladder, slowed by her injured hand. The others were all in the lab before she arrived. Her father's face relaxed when she walked in.

"All right. We were packed up for travel, but not for the shaking we just got. I want everybody in the hold checking on our samples. Make sure they are intact and safely stowed. Pentam, have a look at your darkroom. Cal you're with me. Captain Cully will want to hear from you what happened."

The Captain stood on the bow deck taking reports from the crew.

"All hands present and accounted for." Henrichs spoke in the tones she would have ordered dinner. "Two injuries. One fell down a ladder when the ship heaved. Hit his head, but he'll be fine. The other...." She looked over at Cal and pain crossed her face. "Monky was in the boiler room when we got hit. The stoke door was open. He's burned pretty bad. Purser's with him now.

"Captain." Thomas stepped up. "We've got a problem. That blow to the ship was that bloody big serpent hitting the rudder. It's gone, torn right off."

The Captain went still then nodded his head. "Get a team together and assess the damage. Can we jury-rig something with what we have? Bran?" The assistant engineer stepped forward. "We need that boiler room put to rights. Hop on it."

"I don't know..." Bran trailed off uncertainly.

"I have a schematic that will help. We'll get it done." Cal looked at Captain Cully. "We could use another set of hands." She held hers up.

Captain Cully pointed at a burly sailor, and Cal led them to the ladder down.

"I'll just grab my schematic from my berth, you get down there and check the pressure, better low than high." She left them scrambling down the ladder and ran to fetch her drawing. She made it down the ladders and stepped into the engine room. Coals scattered across the floor. Cal looked at the sailor.

"Derrik, right? Grab the shovel and get that coal back in the fire."

"Yes, ma'am." He picked up the shovel and began clearing the floor.

Cal picked her way over to the boiler.

"Pressure's really low, we must have lost water."

"Let's find where."

Bran and Cal went over the boiler drawing in hand.

"Here, the pressure release took a bang from something." Cal pointed to where the valve was twisted.

"What would be heavy enough to do that?"

Cal pointed to the bulkhead where the massive shaft went through to the ocean.

"The hull twisted when the thing hit, one of the pipes could have hit the valve."

Bran tried turning the valve. It moved a little, then stopped.

"We'll need to replace it."

"We'll have to dump the steam."

"Most of its gone now anyway. You saw the pressure; the pistons aren't moving."

"How are we going to do that?" Bran looked at her wide-eyed. "We aren't even proper engineers."

Cal pointed to the tools. "We have tools. First we cool down, then get the thing off. Have a look and see if the valve is welded or threaded. Pray for threads."

"Yes, ma'am." Bran saluted. Cal stepped out of the engine room and opened the door to where Monky had mentioned spare parts.

"Good Heavens." Cal looked around. There had to be enough to rebuild most of the engine room. Pipes of varying diameters, valves of all kinds and sizes. Even something which looked like a miniature boiler. She couldn't imagine what it was for. There was nothing like it in the engine room. She went back to the engine room.

"Report."

"Coals are cleaned up, ma'am. Bran said to dump water on them, we didn't want them burning right now." Derrick stood at attention.

"Good thinking, Bran."

"The valve is threaded. That wrench," Bran pointed to a massive thing on the wall, held down with chains, "will fit if we kind find a gorilla to use it. I'm checking all the other valves for damage. So far everything looks good."

"Very good, continue. I'm going to report to the Captain."

"Yes, ma'am."

Cal climbed up to the deck and found the Captain with Sir Shillingsworth and Henrichs trying to come up with a solution.

"Assistant Engineer Cal reporting." Cal's hand ached as she tried to salute.

"You've given yourself a promotion." The Captain smiled briefly at her. Cal blushed. "Don't worry, I think I'll make it official. Give your report, engineer."

"Good news and bad news." Cal tried to keep her voice as matter of fact as Henrichs. "The pressure relief valve took a hit and we've lost most of our pressure. We won't be able to replace it until the boiler's cool. I've shut down the fire. We should be able to work on it by tomorrow. Good news is we have plenty of parts, and so far there is no other damage we've detected. We won't know about the engine until we fire it up."

"You've ordered a shut down, and set repair in motion?" Captain Cully's voice sounded strange.

"Should I have checked with you first?" Cal's stomach twisted.

"No, you're the ranking engineer. Do what you need. I don't want to slow you down with asking permission for everything. Get it underway."

161

"We have no steerage." The Captain looked at Henrichs. "If we drift toward the weeds, I'll need volunteers to row to at least hold us steady."

"Yes, Sir."

"So all we need is a way to fix the rudder."

"I didn't see anything large enough in the parts room." Cal tried to envision how to steer the Peregrine with the materials on hand.

"No, we don't have a spare rudder on board." Captain Cully slumped in his chair. "Even when you get the engine running, there is no guarantee we can steer the ship."

"Permission to look in on Monky." Cal's face hurt suddenly.

"You aren't needed in the engine room?" Henrichs looked at her.

"The men know what they need to do."

"Go ahead, and get the Purser to look at your face while you're there."

Cal climbed up to the Infirmary.

"Monky?" Cal stepped in to see him lying on the bed. What she'd taken for a sheet over his face was a towel.

"Still here." Monky's words slurred. "Check the boiler."

"I'm on it, Sir."

"I'm no officer, I work for a living."

"I've never seen someone as tough as this old buzzard." The Purser came in and checked the towels on Monky's face. He changed them, and Cal bit her lip against gasping at the ruin of his face.

"Tell me what...?" Monky's breathing slowed and evened out.

"He's on about as much morphine as I dare give him." The Purser came over and frowned at her. "Something tells me you weren't exactly taking it easy." He pulled the bandage off her face. "Well you haven't pulled any stitches, but the cut is bleeding again. He coated her cheek with ointment and put a new bandage on. "Come up when you've finished in the engine room and I'll change the bandage. Don't want oil or grease in that cut."

Cal walked down to the door out to the deck and couldn't make her feet cross the threshold. She went to her berth. Screaming in frustration would only pull more on the stitches. She snatched up an empty sketchbook and started drawing her fears. Her left hand wasn't fast enough so she switched to her right and welcomed the ache. She made her nightmares real. The sea serpent snatching up Pentam, Thomas, Sam, Monky, her. In excruciating detail, she drew picture after picture. Her pencil broke and the pieces rolled across the floor.

She picked them up and put them in her satchel, then carried the sketchbook with her out onto the deck, up to the bow, where Pentam leaned against the rail. Cal slung the sketchbook as far as she could into the water.

"What are you doing?" Pentam put his arm around her.

"My nightmares came out of the ocean, I'm giving them back." She looked down. "I know it's ridiculous."

"No, it's brave."

Cal leaned her head against him and stared out over the mat. The dying sun backlit the derelict ships.

"Sailing ships have rudders, right?"

"I guess so, they have to steer too."

"I need to talk to the Captain." Cal kissed Pentam on the cheek and headed for the bridge after a detour through her equipment locker.

"Assistant Engineer Cal, reporting to the Captain," she said to the sailor who stood at the door.

"Go ahead." The sailor pushed the door open and Cal walked in. The Captain stood staring out the window with a glass in his hand.

"Hello, Cal." Captain Cully swirled his glass and took a swallow. "What can I do for you?"

"Sailing ships have rudders?"

"Yes, not as big as ours, a lot of them were wood."

Cal unrolled her panorama of the derelict ships. She put her finger on a ship with its bow sunk down almost to the water. From the stern hung a rudder.

"We fetch the rudder from this ship and use it to jury-rig the Peregrine. It isn't as big as the Peregrine's had to have been, but it will work."

"I suppose it's possible, if we can get there and back without the serpent attacking."

"I may have an idea about that too. The fish flapping on the surface is what attracted the serpent. They follow the birds and catch the ones which disturb the water too much."

"So it follows vibration, won't it attack the boat?" The Captain put his glass down.

"I don't think so. It didn't attack the boat before; it doesn't make the right kind of vibration."

"The work on the rudder could attract it. We're in bad enough shape without losing more men."

"I looked in the spare parts room. Pentam talked about coming back with a harpoon gun. I can build one." The parts and process were laid out in her mind like the schematic from the engine room.

"You're going to build one?" The Captain looked at the paper and ran his finger across the pencilled ship.

"Monky gave me the idea. He said if the boiler blew a valve, it would blow a hull right through the ship."

"Saw the results of a boiler explosion once. I can imagine it would generate that kind of force. Draw out your plan, and what you need. We'll look at it in the light of day." Captain Cully picked up his glass. "Do you like brandy, Cal?"

"I've had it once or twice."

Captain Cully poured brandy into a glass and handed it to her.

"Here's to a dead sea serpent." They clinked glasses and Cal sipped at her glass. The brandy burned down to her stomach and warmed her. When she'd finished, she put the glass down and left the bridge. The sailor at the door saluted her as she passed.

Chapter 13 Steam Cannon

"You're going to do what?" Pentam tried to hold his words in, but the fear bubbling in his chest forced its way out.

"Build a steam cannon and use it to kill the sea serpent. Then we'll bring the rudder back to

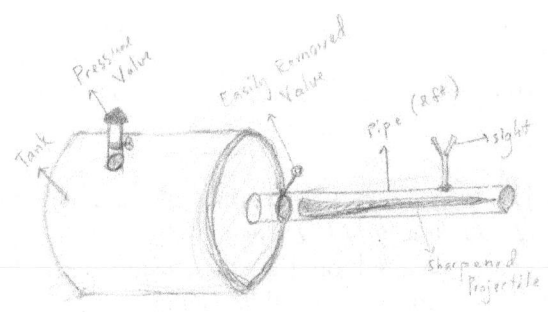

the Peregrine and make the repair." Cal looked at him as if what she described was as simple as going to the market. The bandage on her cheek made her look frail until he met her eyes and saw the indomitable spirit burning there.

"Do you know how dangerous steam cannons are?" Damn, that wasn't what I want to say, traitorous mouth.

"Floating with no rudder isn't safe either." Captain Cully frowned at Pentam.

"But going to the derelicts...." Pentam snapped his mouth shut and left before he said any more. He caught a glimpse of the hurt on Cal's face. Then she dismissed him and turned to the task at hand. Pentam went to the stern rail and looked out over the ocean away from the weeds. He didn't want to see how close they'd drifted.

The discussion on the deck had finished. He'd been the only one foolish enough to hope there might be another way. Sailors opened the hatch behind him. Cal's voice floated up, pointing out what she needed from the cargo hold. It was casual and matter of fact, as if he hadn't just walked away from her. Pain wrenched at his heart and he tried to fight back the sobs.

"The only thing scarier than facing danger is watching someone you love face it."

Henrichs leaned on the rail beside him. "It's why I'm only married to this ship. I couldn't do what you're going to have to do."

"And what would that be?" Pentam's words rasped at his throat. Metal clanged behind him. Men grunted as they lifted heavy objects.

"You're going to kiss her good luck and tell her you trust her." Henrichs left no room for argument. "She can't be distracted by worry about you."

"About me?" Pentam turned to look at Henrichs. It was a mistake. Her eyes bored deep into his soul and pinned him like one of Dan's bugs.

"She loves you, and you ran away leaving her to think you doubt her. You don't think her heart isn't going to be aching? An instant of distraction could be the difference between life and death. If you love her at all, you'll make sure she doesn't have to think about anything but her task. You can melt into a pool of jelly later."

Pentam tried to argue, but now his words caught in his throat. Henrichs didn't expect argument, she expected him to obey. Cal was a member of the crew, Henrich's responsibility.

"Yes, ma'am." He took hold of the fear and strangled it, stuffed it down deep in his soul.

"Good man." Henrichs' face softened and she put her hand on his shoulder briefly.

Pentam turned to see Cal ordering a mix of scientists and crew as they laid out a long pipe in front of a steel barrel. Thomas wielded an immense wrench to attach a fitting to the barrel. Another stepped up to help and both men strained.

"That should be good." Cal pointed at the pipe. "Let's get this on." The group picked up the pipe and Cal guided the end into the threads. They turned it until they couldn't any more, then used the pipe wrench again.

The pipe looked horribly fragile. Pentam envisioned the thing exploding, sending pieces of Cal flying away.

He walked up to the group. Cal looked at him and frowned. A knife went through his heart.

"Maybe a second pipe welded over the first one where the joint is. It needs to withstand a lot of pressure."

Cal considered his suggestion, then nodded to herself.

"Take Stefan and pick out something which will work." A sailor stepped away from the group and Pentam followed him away.

"We'll need a welder. Let's get this ready to put Pentam's pipe in place." Cal's orders followed him through the door.

He climbed down the ladder, then another and another to the depth of the ship. Banging came from the engine room. Pentam peeked in to see two sailors, black with oil and grease struggling with a fitting on the boiler.

In the parts hold, Stefan was already comparing pipes.

"Better to be a bit too big than too small. We can wrap the barrel of the cannon to make the fit tighter." Pentam looked around at the room.

Stefan nodded and slapped a length of pipe. Pentam inspected it, tried to heft it. He struggled to get it off the floor before his hands slipped.

"The cannon needs to be a balance between strength and weight. It's no good if they can't get it into place."

Stefan nodded again, then wrapped a length of chain around the pipe. He whistled sharply. A head appeared in the hatch far above. The rope was lowered for them to fasten to the chain. A minute later the pipe lifted off the floor and up to the deck.

"Thanks," Pentam said to Stefan. "You go back up on deck. I'm going see if I can't lend a hand in the engine room." He rolled up his sleeves and went to the other room.

"Anything I can do to help?"

Within minutes he was black with oil and grease and thinking about nothing but forcing a recalcitrant fitting into place.

***

Cal inspected the finished cannon. The double walled barrel added a lot of weight, but Pentam was right. The release valve had been fitted so she could attach a long bar to it for leverage. She wouldn't have time to wrestle with it. Her arm was greased to the shoulder from trying to get it to move easily.

The harpoon was an eight-foot length of oak which fit exactly into the barrel. The crew had dulled a couple of axes and several knives putting a wicked point on it. Thomas had used a rag on a stick to oil the inside of the barrel after packing it with wads of canvas.

She saw the force her cannon would generate. Nothing made of flesh and blood would survive a direct hit.

It weighed too much. All of them together couldn't move the blasted thing. They could use the crane to load it in the boat, but how were they going to get it in position? Thomas said he could do it. She trusted him.

Henrichs announced she was coming, and to Cal's shock, her father insisted on coming as well. Captain Cully had dug up a sword for him, and she remembered Henrichs saying how good he was with it.

"We go as soon as we can get the boat loaded." Cal peered up at the sun and frowned. She didn't want to be wrestling with this beast at night. It would take some time to fill the tank, and more to heat it up to a decent pressure. She ran calculations in her head. It would mean the middle of the night at the earliest they would have enough pressure.

"You'll need two boats." Henrichs eyed the cannon. "The second one can return after everything is transferred to the derelict."

"You heard her," Cal shouted, "let's get the boats in the water. Everything but the cannon in the small boat. Load it first and stand off. We load the cannon in the larger one. Only the rowers in with the cannon. My father and I will ride in the second." She looked around. "Where's Pentam?"

Stefan pointed down.

"He's still down there? What's he doing?"

Stefan pantomimed using a wrench.

"I'll be back in a few minutes. Henrichs, if you can take over here?"

The First Mate nodded with a slight smile, and Cal ran off.

In the engine room, Pentam and Derick struggled with a pipe while Bran guided it into the fitting.

"There." Bran dropped down to the floor, while Pentam and Derik slumped. "We'll have to weld it."

"We're finished on deck. Get it welded and start the fire. The sooner we have pressure the better. I want us to be able to sail as soon as the rudder's in place." Cal looked closely at the fitting.

"Aye, aye, ma'am." Pentam's eyes twinkled at her through the black on his face. He pushed himself off the floor and came over to her while Bran headed up to the deck.

173

Cal used her sleeve to wipe the worst of the mess from Pentam's mouth, then kissed him soundly, tasting him, memorizing the feel of his body against hers. Reluctantly she stepped back.

"I must go."

"I know." Pentam reached to caress her unbandaged cheek. "I wouldn't want to be that sea serpent." He grinned, but Cal saw the glisten in his eyes and felt the trembling of his arms.

"In my satchel there's a spyglass, if you want to watch over me."

"I'm sorry—"

Cal put a finger over his lips. "I know." She turned and left the engine room before the tears started in her eyes.

Chapter 14 Night Battle

The boat bumped up against the derelict. Sir Shillingsworth jumped out and fastened the rope, then helped Cal on board. The rowers handed them the bags of coal and the thin metal sheathing Cal hoped would shield the deck long enough to get the cannon up to pressure. Last came a mess of rope and blocks Thomas had put in the boat.

"All right, get back to the ship before dark. You were fine all the way here; you'll be safe on the way back."

The sailors saluted, then spun the boat and headed back. The large boat moved into place; Cal and her father took the ropes. She watched how Sir Shillingsworth fastened his rope and copied him. Thomas leaped onto the derelict and looked up the mast. He climbed up carrying the blocks and rope on his back.

"Let's get the shield in place." Cal picked up one side, her father the other. They half-carried, half-dragged it through the tangle of weeds covering the deck. Sir Shillingsworth cut away the weeds near the mast and they settled the shield in place. Cal found pieces of wood to put under it, and when it was steady she emptied two bags of coal onto it and spread it out. She looked up at Thomas.

"Ready?"

"There's a spare here I can rig the blocks to." He tied them in position with heavy rope, then dropped the other rope which he'd fed through the main block. Instead of climbing down the mast, he slid down the ropes. Over on the boat, he fastened the smaller blocks to the chains welded in place on the cannon. He took one rope and Henrichs the other, pulling them through until they were tight.

Cal got a complete picture of the principles in her head. The more blocks the less strength to pull the rope, but much more rope to haul.

Cal and her father went to help. They had to pull a lot of rope through the block and tackle to move the cannon, but as she expected the weight wasn't unmanageable. The ungainly thing dragged over the gunwale of the boat, letting water into the boat before scraping on the deck. As it got closer to the mast, it lifted and swung until it hung over the shield.

They lowered it into place. Only a foot or so of space separated it from the massive wood mast. The mast would be enough to stop the cannon when it fired. Thomas unhooked the ropes from the tank then moved the chains so he could fasten ropes to them. He found solid places to tie the block, then tightened the ropes until creaking made Cal wave.

The cannon squatted on the deck aiming down toward the water.

"Can we lift the barrel a bit more?" Cal sighted down it. "I don't want to hit the water with the harpoon; it will bounce."

The other three hauled on the ropes holding the barrel pulling it up until Cal waved her hand.

"Tie it off. Any further, we'll bend the barrel." She lifted the bar she had fitted to work the valve. With the wrench, she tightened the bolts holding it, then Thomas cranked it further. Her father poured oil over the coal and lit it while Henrichs filled a bucket of water to start filling the tank.

The sun dropped below the horizon as the four demolished the food cook had sent with them. Coals glowed red under the tank. The pressure gauge started to move upward.

An oar had been rigged on a rope to splash on the surface in line with the barrel of the steam cannon.

"We'll need to take turns watching the pressure. From the thickness and weight of the tank we should aim for 250 psi before firing the cannon. As soon as we get close to pressure we'll start on the oar to call the serpent."

"Yes, ma'am." Henrichs said.

"You don't need to say that." Cal flushed. "I'm not even a full engineer."

"On this ship, you're Captain." Henrichs gave a twisted grin. "Though I have to say, I've seen nicer ships."

"All right." Cal closed her eyes and focused. She let the plan flow through her mind like pencil on paper. *I'm insane, Pentam was right.* "Henrichs, take first watch. Father, second. Wake me as soon as the pressure gets to 200. Thomas pull up doors, hatches whatever and make a shield between the cannon and the stern deck. No one goes near the tank once it reaches 100 psi. If it blows, it will be at the valve and the mast will take most of the damage. If the deck under the cannon starts smoking, run water beneath it. It wouldn't be a bad idea to run a bucket under it every so often anyway."

"Anything I'm missing?"

"Weapons." Sir Shillingsworth slapped his sword. "With luck, we won't need them."

"Good thinking." Cal put her fingers to her forehead.

"I have my harpoon with me." Henrichs picked her way to the boat and lifted it out. She tossed a hook on a three-foot handle to Thomas.

Henrichs pointed at Cal. "You're the one running the cannon. Focus on that."

Cal nodded, but found a stick and laid it down beside her. She didn't think she'd sleep, but her eyes closed as soon as her head hit her arm.

***

Sir Shillingsworth watched his daughter sleep. He tried to remember when he was that young. It would have been his second trip out with Harrison. The old man put up with his naïve ideas. Harrison would have loved Cal, but he was lost when his ship went down in the icy polar sea.

Sir Shillingsworth had always been proud of Cal, bragging about her artistic ability, using her drawings in his presentations. She'd charmed Lord Carroway, won over the entire crew of the Peregrine, shaken up the hotel in Finches Harbour. He doubted she had any awareness of her impact on the people around her.

Mary, you wouldn't have been surprised at all. Wish I'd been there more for the both of you.

"Better follow the Captain's orders." Sir Shillingsworth leaned against the mast, the sword close at hand. Henrichs smiled and poured water beneath the shield.

***

Cursing woke Cal. She rolled to her feet with her club in hand and took in the surroundings. Thomas battled something toward the stern. The moon lit the ship in start black and white.

179

"Crabs," Henrichs said and pointed. The rail of the ship was covered with them.

"We can't let them take over." Cal hefted her club. "You take starboard, Father the port, I'll go help Thomas. Keep an eye on the pressure." She glanced at the gauge. 150; they'd be OK for a bit.

"Bloody big crab jumped up and bit me." Thomas waved a bloody hand at Cal.

"Go back to the cannon, watch the gauge, keep the fire hot." She tossed her club to him and he threw the hook to her. A crab scuttled toward her and she swung the hook, flipping it back onto the other crabs. They swarmed it, but some still came at her. Cal batted at the things; their size slowed them down. They were top heavy, a good blow just under the front of the shell was enough to send them flying. If the blow didn't kill them, the rest of the mob did.

She swung the boat hook until her arms were leaden. Shouts from around the cannon told her the others were just as busy.

"200 psi." Henrichs shouted.

"I'm coming, Father switch with me." Cal turned and ran back to the cannon, passing Sir Shillingsworth, covered with bits of crab, but still holding his sword firmly.

A crab, bigger than the others headed for the cannon, pincers waving. It caught one of the ropes holding the cannon steady and sliced through it like it was thread. Cal brought the boat hook down on the crab's shell and flattened it to the deck, then she kicked it down to where the bow met the black water. It flipped over the edge, but one leg caught as it struggled to get free; the rest of the horde turned and scuttled away.

A ping from the tank made Cal look at it in horror.

"Get back, now, it's deforming. It will blow any second."

The gauge read 260 psi.

The crab had stopped struggling. *Need to see.* Cal batted at the coals sending them scattering across the deck toward the bow. The tinder dry wood caught fire. The flame's red light reflected off the wet black skin of the sea serpent. Cal snatched up the rope to fire the cannon, but the serpent was too far on the other side. Cal ran to starboard, waving and screaming. The huge head snapped around like a pointing hound. Lines and curves screamed through her mind, changing as the monster moved. Then everything fell into place.

Cal ran behind the mast as the creature's head lunged forward. It hit the mast as Cal rolled on the deck and hauled on the rope.

The cannon thundered. The entire ship shook and moved back in the water. Cal didn't see the harpoon move. One second the serpent was tearing at the mast, the next a hole appeared in its body, a little above the water line. The sea serpent collapsed to the deck, then slid off into the water, dragging the cannon with it. Her mind had told her the force it would have; she hadn't comprehended what it meant.

"Report." Cal croaked out from where she lay on the deck.

"Henrichs here."

"Thomas."

Cal sat up ignoring the twinges and aches.

"Father?" She shouted as loud as she could. A moan came from further to the stern.

"I've got him," Henrichs called. "He's battered, but breathing. I can't tell anything else in the dark."

"I didn't think to bring a lantern." Cal cursed herself, then flames erupted and Thomas held up a chunk of wood with burning cloth on the end.

"You'll need a new tool bag."

They gathered around Sir Shillingsworth. One leg twisted under him. Cal couldn't see if he was bleeding. Thomas handed Cal the torch and helped Henrichs roll Sir Shillingsworth on his side. By torchlight, Henrichs set the leg and bound it between two pieces of rail.

"God, I could use a drink." Henrichs flopped down on the deck beside Sir Shillingsworth. Cal sat on the other side while Thomas kept the torch burning and watched over them.

"We don't appear to be sinking," he said.

"Good, I don't want to have done this for nothing." Cal put her head back. "Good work, crew. We should stand watches for the rest of the night. Thomas, take first watch. Wake me if the ship sinks."

Chapter 15 Limping to Port

The boom thundered from the darkness hiding the derelict ship. Pentam cursed as he tried to see through the spyglass, but it only magnified the black void.

Others lined the rail with him, watching, praying. A cheer went up when a speck of light appeared.

"Someone's moving over there." Dr. Franklyn said.

Pentam put the useless glass in his pocket, then stood watch at the rail. The others gradually faded away, back to duty or bed. He stood staring at the tiny flickering light until the sun burst from the ocean.

"Make ready the boats." Captain Cully bellowed. Sailors scurried to get them ready. They loaded one with tools, Captain Cully climbed in the other. "You coming?" He looked back at Pentam.

Pentam scrambled into the boat and they rowed off toward the ships. He jumped aboard the wreck as soon as the boat nudged it.

"Permission to come aboard." Captain Cully stood in the row boat, a crooked smile on his face.

"Permission granted." Cal sounded exhausted, but she leaped to her feet to catch Pentam in a long kiss. The sailors swarmed over the ship to work on the rudder. The two smaller boats were tied together to hold it.

Something glinted in the sunlight, stuck in the mast. Pentam used the boat hook to pull down an enormous tooth.

"Cal." Pentam caught her attention. She came over from where she'd been sitting with Sir Shillingsworth. "I think you deserve this." He put the tooth in her hands. She needed both to hold it. For a long moment, they stared at the thing, then Cal handed it back.

"Hold onto it for me?" Pentam took it, and watched her as she sat beside her father. Sir Shillingsworth groaned and she immediately sat up.

"Father?"

"I'm guessing, from the fact I'm still alive, that you were successful."

"*We* were." Cal squeezed his hand. "I couldn't have done without you."

"Cal, I'd like to get your father back to the ship." Henrichs crouched down beside them. "They'll be a while getting that rudder off."

"I should stay..." Cal trailed off and looked at Sir Shillingsworth. "Please let Captain Cully know I'm heading back."

Henrichs stood and saluted. "Aye, aye, ma'am."

A group of sailors hoisted Sir Shillingsworth and carried him to the boat. Pentam climbed in to sit with Cal, who sat on the bottom of the boat with her father's head in her lap. Stefan and another sailor climbed in and set out off to the Peregrine.

**

Cal sat beside her father in the infirmary sketching the battle with the crabs and the sea monster. She'd filled most of the sketchbook. Monky slept in the other bed.

"Captain's compliments, he is asking the engineer to report to the bridge." Thomas grinned at her.

"I'll stay with him." Pentam said.

Cal followed Thomas up to the bridge.

"Ah, Engineer, Second Class Shillingsworth, how quickly can you get this tub underway?"

"Bran told me the boiler is holding pressure. We're almost to operational now. I'll get done there and get on it. We'll need to bring it up slow, I don't know what that bulkhead will do to the shaft when we transfer power, and I don't know if there is damage to the engine I can't see."

"Get on it."

Cal headed out, sticking her head in the door to tell Pentam where she was heading, then she ran to her berth, put her engine-room clothes on and slid down the ladder.

Bran waited for her.

"Pressure's at 50 psi." He shrugged. "You hear that whistle? Don't think we'll get much higher without blowing the valve."

"Fifty it is then. I'm going to check the pistons one last time then we'll set the engine going." Cal climbed through to the huge pistons. She didn't see any dents or material caught in the arms, but globbed some grease about for good measure. "Start the pressure to the engine. Take it slow, and be ready to cut back at my shout."

"Yes, ma'am."

A hiss told her he'd opened the valve.

"Earplugs!" she shouted, then put hers in. The engine strained, and Cal almost yelled for him to cut the steam then the pistons clanged and the drive arms started moving.

"Increase pressure feed to one half."

"One half."

The shaft turned faster and the deck beneath her feet vibrated.

"Slowly bring pressure feed to three quarters."

The vibration changed and the shaft thumped.

"Hold." Cal shouted. "Back it off." The shaft slowed and the thumping vanished.

"That's it." Cal climbed back to Bran. She looked at the valve. "We're running at a little less than two thirds power. Report to the Captain, I'll take this shift."

"Aye, aye, ma'am." Bran saluted and headed out of the room.

Cal felt the vibration of the room, then backed off the speed a bit further. The bell from the bridge rang twice in acknowledgement. Cal spent her watch letting her mind calculate their speed and how much coal and water they'd need. They'd make it to Finches Harbour, but slow.

When Bran relieved her, Cal staggered up to her berth and barely had energy to clean up before falling into bed. The giant tooth lay on her pillow. Cal stuffed it into her satchel and forgot it.

Thomas woke her in time for breakfast and her next shift.

"Cal, you're pushing yourself too hard." Pentam sat down beside her. "Can't someone run the engine room?"

"Who?" Cal looked at him, too tired to argue. "Are you going to help? We could use another hand."

Pentam opened his mouth, then closed it and looked down.

"I love you, Pentam, but don't get in the way when I have a job to do." Cal pushed herself to her feet and headed down to the engine room. She brushed tears from her eyes, then pushed away all thought but getting the Peregrine back to Finches Harbour

***

They limped into port at one quarter power with the shaft hammering the engine room. Listening to the engine struggle brought tears to Cal's eyes. The machine had struggled mightily to get them here, but it wasn't going any further. The signal from the bridge came to shut down the engine. Cal cut the steam and killed the fire. Whatever they did to this ship, the engine room would need to be completely refitted.

Cal headed upstairs. She watched at the rail while two of the boats rowed the Peregrine to the dock. She didn't leave her spot until the ropes were secured and the gangplank down. While the team left the ship, headed for the hotel, Cal went to check on her father and Monky.

"Hear ye're a proper engineer now, Cal." Monky sat up in his bed.

"There's so much you never showed me." Cal sat beside him.

"It'll come, som'un 'll teach you."

"Thanks, Monky." She patted his hand and stepped over to her father's bed.

"This blasted leg itches."

"So you've told me. Dr. Franklyn said he'd arrange for you to be transferred to the hotel. It will be a bit more comfortable there."

"Thank you, dear. How's Pentam?"

"He's trying, but he's determined to get between me and what I have to do." Cal had stopped shedding tears over it as the engine consumed her attention.

"How are you?"

"More scared about how I'm going to tell him. I still love him; I don't think I could live with him."

Her father squeezed her hand.

"Better go get changed and head up to the hotel. I'll be fine for now."

"I will see you there."

Cal went to her berth. For a moment, she considered going and fetching the gown, but that felt like lying to Pentam. Instead she put on her clean dress and put her satchel over her shoulder. Time to face the inevitable.

Surely if she could face the sea serpent, she could talk to Pentam.

***

Pentam walked into the hotel and headed straight to his room. He ordered a bath, then chose his clothes when his luggage arrived. After an hour of scrubbing, Pentam climbed out of the bath and dressed in the finest clothes he'd brought with him. They'd be here a while, and he didn't want to look less than a gentleman. The hotel was almost full so the team had to share rooms. Sir Shillingsworth would join Pentam as soon as they got him transferred.

He strolled down to the lounge and sat at a table with Dr. Franklyn and Prof. Orthin.

"So now what?" Pentam waved down a waiter and ordered a glass of wine. "I can't imagine the Peregrine can be fixed any time soon. Do we wait here for months?"

"There is another ship in port, a luxury ship. If they have space, we could return on it, commission a ship to come and collect the research and specimens from the Peregrine. Everything will be in the city in a couple of months. It will take months after that to catalog, analyze and write a report on our findings." Prof. Orthin swirled his glass and sighed. "There are worse places to be stuck than here."

Dr. Franklyn shook his head.

"Tempting, but I do have responsibilities in the city. I for one, will be talking to the Captain of the Demeter about booking passage home."

Lahdin slid into a seat across from Pentam.

"I think I will remain a while, maybe return on the ship which brings parts for the Peregrine. This island must be a treasure trove of insect life. I'll let Dan decide for himself, but I'm hoping he will stay with me."

They ordered a meal and talked about the trip and what they might present when they reached home.

Pentam watched for Cal to arrive. A woman walked in, dressed in a fine gown; for a moment he thought it was Cal, but her blonde hair cascaded down her back in artfully curled waves. She walked in a way which informed all watching that she'd grown up with such finery.

A table of older people welcomed her.

"Miss Crysabel Dimant, daughter of a Baron who, according to her, has his estate too far from anything interesting. Meaning I think, fashion and men." Cal sat beside Pentam. She had the strangest smile on her face.

"How on earth do you know all that?" Dr. Franklyn turned to look across at the young woman.

"Señor Calamphi was very apologetic, but there are simply no suitable rooms left. Miss Dimant was kind enough to allow me to share hers."

"How is Sir Shillingsworth?" Pentam put the girl out of his mind and turned to Cal.

"Cranky." Cal grinned broadly. "The hotel has called in a surgeon who admitted the leg was set tolerably well under the circumstances. It's too late to do anything about it now. He's to start putting a little weight on it tomorrow, so I expect you'll see him dashing about the hotel."

"Did you bring your gown to the hotel?" Pentam put his hand on hers. "I would love to see you in it again."

"I'll be meeting with the engineer from the other ship all day tomorrow to do an assessment of the damage. Captain Cully would like to send a list of the parts we need back with this ship."

"We're in port, can't you let someone else do that?" Pentam would have taken back his words, but they rang out through the lounge making everyone turn and look at him.

"We'll be here a while." Cal's expression didn't change. "There will be time for us to spend together." She waved down a waiter. "I'll have a brandy, please, the best you have available."

"When did you start drinking brandy?" Prof. Orthin spoke up quickly as if he knew the question was on Pentam's lips.

"Captain Cully and I shared a toast to the destruction of the sea serpent."

"At least you've ordered the best." Pentam sighed.

***

By the time Pentam got up, Cal had broken her fast and gone down to the Peregrine. He sat at a table in the corner and sipped at his tea.

"You must be Pentam Booksdale." A lilting voice lifted him from his sulk. "Calliope told me you knew your way around town and might show me the sights." He looked up to see Miss Dimant standing, somewhat uncertainly. "You must think me terribly forward." She turned red. "I'm sorry to have bothered you."

"No, wait." Pentam stood and pulled out a chair. "I apologize, I am not nearly awake yet."

"Calliope did say you had quite an adventure?" She leaned toward him. "I didn't understand any of the science, though she said she couldn't talk about most of it."

"Yes, well, we sailed to the Sargasso Sea on a scientific expedition. Most of it wasn't that exciting, crabs and fish, and lots of seaweed. We had engine trouble and had to limp back to port."

"That must have been horrible."

"It gave us time to read our notes over a great deal."

Miss Dimant laughed.

"Now tell me about this divine shop Calliope mentioned."

After tea, Pentam called a cart and helped Crysabel into the seat then jumped up beside her.

"The market please, Joliu, you know the one. Miss Calliope asked me to show her friend around the town."

Crysabel *oohed* and *aahed* as they passed the sights.

"Please, can we drive about the market? I was never allowed in a market like this. Mother worried I'd be kidnapped and she'd never see me again."

"Joliu will keep you safe." Pentam nodded to the man, who nodded back.

"And you too, surely?"

"I will talk chemistry to them until they die of boredom."

Crysabel's laugh echoed through the market and people turned to point to her. She waved back smiling brightly and Joliu started off at a walk. The girl admired the work at the booths and wistfully looked at a tray of necklaces made from brightly coloured feathers.

"Mother would never let me wear them, but they are so beautiful."

Pentam hopped out of the cart and went to talk to the woman selling the necklaces. He negotiated briefly, then picked out one made with the brightest shades of blue. Climbing back up he handed it to her.

"I wasn't sure which you liked, but this matches your eyes. You don't need to wear it to enjoy it."

"Oh, but I must wear it. She lifted her hair out of the way. Please put it on."

Pentam tied the thong for her and she let her hair fall. "How does it look?"

He had to swallow to get the words out. Her eyes were so open and filled with wonder.

"It is beautiful."

"Mother will be furious." Crysabel sounded pleased at the prospect.

They meandered through the market. Crysabel wouldn't eat any of the food sold there, but insisted on buying an inordinate amount for some sad-eyed children who had taken to following them. Pentam had her stop at the dress shop where she bought a couple of hats and gifts for her servants back home.

"Tell me about Calliope." Crysabel asked as she finally allowed Joliu to carry them back to the hotel.

"She's a brilliantly talented artist." Pentam smiled. "And she is kind and caring like you. Everyone here calls her Lady Cal because they love her so much."

"You sound like you're in love with her yourself." She lifted a brow at him.

"I just wish she weren't so busy, you'd be fast friends I'm sure."

"What is she so busy at? There's nothing to do on this island."

"She's meeting an engineer about getting the ship fixed."

"Calliope owns the ship?"

"No, she's the ship's engineer."

Crysabel looked at him in disbelief.

"When our ship was damaged, the engineer was hurt. Cal took over and somehow got it back here. I guess she feels obligated to see it repaired properly." Pentam tried to sound proud of her. He should, Cal was an astonishing person, but it didn't come out the way he intended.

Crysabel started giggling, and Pentam's gut twisted. He shouldn't have said anything, now Crysabel wouldn't want to be anywhere near Cal.

"Does she have a uniform?" Crysabel's question pushed all thought out of Pentam's head. "Please tell me she has a uniform. There's a fancy-dress ball next week. Wouldn't it be marvelous if I could go dressed as a sailor?"

"You'd make an impression." Pentam said.

"Oh, you, you're no fun at all."

Chapter 16 Drydock

Cal rode up the hill to the hotel, fuming. The other engineer had been insufferable and refused to talk to her. It took Captain Cully threatening to speak to the man's Captain to get him to look at the engine room at all. Then he had no advice beyond what Cal had already figured out.

Captain Cully was going to talk to the other captains and try to find a more suitable helper. He ordered her to go to the hotel, see her father and Pentam, and rest.

The cart let her off at the door and Cal stalked into the hotel. Everyone in the lobby turned to stare.

Oh, for goodness sake, it's only a bit of honest grime.

Señor Calamphi ran out to meet her.

"Lady Cal, I will send hot water up to your room immediately. Is there anything else you require?"

"I haven't eaten all day, Señor. Whatever the kitchen has hot would be wonderful. Send it up in an hour, if you would."

"Yes, Lady Cal." He bowed, then clapped his hands sharply giving orders to the men as he walked back to the desk.

Cal climbed the stairs after making sure she wasn't leaving greasy footprints behind her. A room on the fourth floor had a lovely view, but too many stairs after a long day.

Meireka met her at the door to the room she shared with Crysabel.

"Lady, the other girl is sleeping. Go to the bath, and I will carry the water to you so the men don't enter the room."

"Thank you, Meireka. You are very thoughtful." Cal opened the door and tried to walk through the room silently.

"Oh!" The girl on the bed sat up and stared wide-eyed at Cal. "Pentam said you were an engineer. I hardly believed him. You must be exhausted. I'll ring for a bath."

"Thank you, but Señor Calamphi has already told the men to bring the water. Meireka will carry it through the room for modesty's sake."

"Meireka?"

"The maid, she asked to work our room specially." Cal headed for the bathroom. Crysabel followed her.

"Mother made me pack so many soaps and bath oils, as if we couldn't get more on our trip. What do you like? I have lavender and rose, here's some cedar, and pine."

"Pine would be nice, and it helps take the oil off."

"Really?" Crysabel handed her a bottle. "It reminds me too much of home."

Meireka appeared with the first bucket.

"It would be a pity to get the bathwater all oily. I could help you rinse the worst off while they bring the rest of the water." Crysabel looked worried, as if she was crossing some boundary.

"That would be wonderful." Cal unfastened her shirt and pulled it off, then her pants. Meireka swooped them up and vanished. "I hope she doesn't get all oily from them."

Crysabel had removed her outer dress. She poured water over Cal, who soaped her arms and face. She didn't feel uncomfortable at all in her smallclothes with this girl. By the time Meireka had carried the rest of the buckets in, Crysabel pronounced Cal fit to climb into the tub.

Cal removed the last of her clothes and settled into the hot water with a sigh. Crysabel poured a little of the pine oil into the tub, then worked away at Cal's hair.

"What happened to your face? I can't see it except up close, but that scar looks terrifying."

"You should have seen it before the Purser stitched it up. Let's just say swimming through seaweed with a knife in your teeth is not a good idea."

"Really?" Crysabel paused in her cleaning of Cal's hair.

"I wouldn't recommend it."

"But you got the scar from the knife?"

"Actually, I don't know. It might have been the knife, or the seaweed. Some of it had a nasty edge."

"You must have been petrified."

"It wasn't the worst thing that could have happened."

Crysabel took up washing hair again.

"I always loved taking baths when I was young. Nurse would make sure I came out clean. She always did my hair. Nurse died just before we left on the trip. I missed her ever so much."

"Tell me about your trip." Cal leaned back and let Crysabel have her way.

"We traveled by train and ship so many places I've lost count. All the hotels were the same. I mean Father's a Baron, so we need to keep up appearances, but none of it felt like an adventure. Not really. I had more fun with your friend, Pentam, this afternoon than I had in all the months we've been away. This is our last stop. After the costume ball, we'll be leaving for home."

"What did you think of the dress shop?"

"I was so disappointed; they didn't have a gown ready. You made it sound so lovely, but Pentam suggested I buy gifts for the servants. That was so much fun, and I bought two hats which are just darling. Pentam bought me a necklace made of blue feathers. He said it matched my eyes. I'll show it to you later. Are you sure it's all right for me to spend time with him?"

"You will be saving him from boredom. He can't spend all day working on his report."

"He's a scientist?" Crysabel said it in the same tone she might have said *unicorn.*

Cal laughed.

"Yes, and a very good one too. He worked on chemistry and helped collect samples. He's very clever."

"He did say something about chemistry and boring people to death."

"That's Pentam. He's worked with my father for the last few years."

"Your father?"

"Sir Shillingsworth."

"I know him!" Crysabel splashed water on Cal's hair. "You better just dunk."

Cal dropped under the water and shook her head. When she came up Crysabel wrapped her hair in a towel.

"I shouldn't say I know your father, but I saw all the cards at the museum with his name on them. It must have been so exciting going on all those adventures."

"This was my first one," Cal said. "The rest of the time I stayed at home to catalog all the specimens and artifacts he brought home."

"But even that must have been something. To handle things from all over the world."

"It was. It made me happy to help him, and you're right, it felt a little like sharing his adventure."

"So why did you come on this trip?" Crysabel massaged Cal's shoulder. "Mother tells me I have magic fingers. She won't let anyone else massage her."

"Ahh, I believe she's right." Cal closed her eyes. "I drew a portrait of Lord Carroway, and he insisted I go."

Crysabel helped her out of the bath and wrapped her in a dressing gown.

"Where did the daughter of a Baron learn to give such wonderful baths?" Cal lay on the bed.

"There's an orphanage in the village not far from my father's mansion. I used to sneak out and help give the children baths. Nurse knew, but kept my secret from my parents. I wonder if the children miss me."

"I'm sure they do."

A knock on the door interrupted them.

"Lady Cal, I've brought your supper."

"Bring it in Meireka." Cal pushed herself up and went to sit in a chair next to a table. Meireka brought in a tray loaded with food.

"Cook didn't know what you wanted, so he sent a little of everything."

"Thank him for me, this looks delicious." Cal waved at Crysabel. "You may as well join me." Cal put a hand on Meireka's arm. "How's Cericia?"

"Oh, she's such a mischief maker. She brings in banana leaves and scribbles on them with sticks from the fire. I get home and she's soot from head to toe. I think she does it just to have a bath every night."

"I'll have to come up and visit again. I had so much fun last time."

"Señor Calamphi is like a different man, he was always grumpy, always worried the guests would get mad. Now he is like everyone's father. Even the laundry maids sing at work. And the guests are happy too. Just ring when you've done with the tray." Meireka curtseyed to Cal and Crysabel.

"What a delightful woman." Crysabel helped herself to some food. "And so beautiful. How lucky you could meet her daughter."

Cal ate until she was comfortably full and could hardly keep her eyes open. Crysabel rang for Meireka.

"Please don't let all this go to waste. Give it to the laundry maids or something."

"Thank you, Miss." Meireka picked up the tray and left.

Cal crawled into bed and dropped off immediately.

***

The sunlight woke Cal. She sat up and looked around. Crysabel still slept soundly. The girl wasn't at all what Cal had expected. She hoped they could stay friends. Meireka or another maid had dropped off Cal's work clothes just inside the door. She dressed quickly then headed down for a quick breakfast before returning to the Peregrine.

"I thought I told you to rest." Captain Cully tried and failed to look severe.

"I did rest, now I'm back to work."

"None of the other engineers know any more than to keep the pressure up and which valves to open. They run the engines, but know nothing about how they work."

"You said you knew your way around an engine room. We can figure it out between the two of us."

"You win. It's that or drink all day." Captain Cully went to get changed while Cal visited Monky.

"We're trying to figure out how to fix the engine." Cal told him. "The boiler's solid, I've been over it a dozen times, but we're losing pressure. I thought it was only the release valve, but I think it must be somewhere else too. I think the shaft is bent. Or the bulkhead is rubbing on it."

205

"Which is it?"

"The shaft." Cal shook her head. "If it was rubbing, it would have screeched."

"I could feel the old girl thumping from up here, even in my dreams." Monky held his hand out shaking it violently.

"I don't know how to fix it."

"If you can't fix it, you'll have to reinvent it. Every engine's a little different. Stop trying to put the old one back together."

"Captain Cully won't let me do that." Cal rubbed her eyes.

"Do what?" Captain Cully stepped in the room in a set of grubby whites.

"She needs to strip the beast down and build it back her way. You won't get no one who can tell ye how, not here anyway."

"We'd better get to work." Captain Cully stepped back.

"Talk to you later, Monky."

"Why? Help me down there. I'd prefer the smell of the engine room over this place."

Cal left the Captain to help Monky dress and climbed down into the engine room. She prowled through it labeling each pipe and valve and engine part in her mind. When she looked at it as a fresh task, not a repair, Cal could see what she'd do differently. How she might make it more efficient.

The Captain came in and set Monky in the corner on a tool box.

"Well?"

"We need to strip the boiler, everything except the water feed for now. Then take apart the engine. Something in it is broken from the wobble on the shaft. I think I can make it more efficient anyway. All that will give me space to get proper pistons and drive arms. I have no idea how we're going to tackle that, but we take it apart first."

Cal wrestled with the wrench while the Captain helped. Each piece they removed, they carried to the part room where they could be winched up on deck.

"Shouldn't have let all those strong young sailors go on shore leave." Captain Cully stretched.

"Not much room for them to work. We'll need them when we start putting it back together."

"You sure you can do that?"

"Little late to ask now, Cap'n," Monky said.

"I've got the schematic to follow." Cal tapped her head. "I know what I need, but I'm going to set it up a bit differently. For one, so Bran doesn't bang his head so much."

Cal headed back up the hill. This time she used the back entrance and the servant's stairs. Meireka came and promised to have the bath ready in no time.

The bath with the pine oil refreshed her, so Cal decided to go down to the lounge to eat. She put on her once-best dress and headed down.

The lounge was crowded with people drinking and laughing, but Cal found a corner in the back to sit. The waiter brought her a brandy and promised food shortly. The brandy warmed her as Cal looked at the people who traveled the world by going from one hotel to the other. She empathized with Crysabel's sadness at not really seeing anything in spite of her travels. Cal had a hard time imagining enjoying travel other than what she had on the Peregrine.

Pentam and Crysabel walked in laughing at something. Cal felt a pang through her heart. They looked good together. Crysabel saw Cal and dragged Pentam over.

"Cal," she said breathlessly when they'd sat, "How did the engineering go today?"

"We decided to strip everything down and rebuild it. There are some improvements I'd like to put in."

"How are you going to do that in a week?" Pentam looked at Cal his brows drawn down in puzzlement.

Cal wanted to smooth the wrinkles away. No, she wanted to grab him by the ears and give him a kiss to scandalize everyone in the room. Instead she smiled.

"I'm staying until the work's done. Father says they're sending a ship to pick up the specimens and equipment. They'll bring me the parts I need."

208

"But your drawing, the report, Lord Carroway." Pentam's face looked about to crumple.

"Pentam, I'm trusting you to bring the journal to Lord Carroway. I'll send it back with the other cargo. You and the others are the scientists. You'll be fine without me."

He pushed away from the table and stalked out of the room.

Cal put her head down and groaned.

"Are you all right?" Crysabel put her hand on Cal's arm.

"No," Cal said into the table cloth, "I'll never be all right."

The food arrived, but Cal's appetite had vanished. Crysabel had them send it up to the room.

"Pentam was supposed to ask you, but I expect he hasn't." Crysabel stood behind Cal in their room, rubbing the tension from her shoulders. "Do you have a uniform? We're about the same size. I think it would be fun to go to the fancy dress ball as a sailor."

"You saw me last night, that's as close to a uniform as I get. You'd terrify them."

"It might be worth it." Crysabel said.

"I don't think so." Cal took one of Crysabel's hands and pulled her around in front. "Sit." She pointed at the other chair. The girl sat with a natural grace, and bit of a pout on her lips.

"You want adventure, you want to rebel against all the things which keep you from living that adventure. But it isn't that easy. I visited the engine room out of boredom. Then a man was killed horribly. I started helping out seriously because I could, and there was no one else." Cal's lips quirked. "I never had a problem getting dirty, much to my mother and father's dismay. Anyway, they trained another man to do the job and I went back to being an artist. Then when our ship got damaged, another man was hurt. A friend of mine. He's blind from being knocked face first onto hot coals."

Crysabel gasped and put her hand to her mouth.

"That's terrible, the poor man."

"It meant I needed to go back to work in the engine room, even though Pentam was terrified I'd be the next one. When I wouldn't listen, he got angry. He's still angry."

"But you love each other! I can hear in how he talks about you. I can see it in your eyes now." Crysabel's own eyes glistened with tears.

"We do." Cal sighed and rubbed her eyes. "Sometimes it isn't enough."

"That's so sad." The girl pulled out a lace handkerchief and dabbed at her eyes. Then leaned over and hugged Cal tight.

***

Cal worked on the engine room every day until it looked naked.

"Tomorrow, I'll look at the shaft. I need something as straight as you can find it, and one or two muscular sailors wouldn't hurt. We're going to turn the shaft by hand."

They'd finished earlier than usual. Cal washed up as much as possible, then picked up a couple of things from the cargo hold.

"Captain Cully, is there a uniform for an engineer?"

"Monky never asked for one, but that doesn't mean we can't make one up. What is this about?"

"There's a fancy-dress ball tomorrow night. I thought a formal uniform would be interesting."

"Let's go raid the Purser's stores."

"He won't be happy." Cal held her hands up.

"I'm the Captain, he'll have to live with it."

Cal shrugged and followed the captain. They found innumerable sets of whites and Cal found a set which fit well enough. The captain dug up a blue jacket.

"Try this on."

"Not bad." Cal moved her arms around. "This could work."

"Needs some insignia. Come to the bridge."

Cal followed him. He was digging around in a drawer when she stepped onto the bridge.

"Ah here it is. Good thing I'm sentimental." Captain Cully held up a pin. A tiny pair of gears hung from a bar. All of it in gold. "The engineer before Monky wore this on his dress uniform. Poor blighter caught some sickness and died. Had no family so most of his stuff was tossed. I kept this to remember him. That was my first steamship."

The Captain stepped forward and pinned it to Cal's jacket.

"Been meaning to make that Engineer Second Class official, but I think I'll skip it. Wear it in good health, Engineer First Class Cal Shillingsworth." Captain Cully saluted and Cal returned it. "Engineers never could salute worth a damn." The Captain enfolded Cal in a powerful hug.

He stepped back and looked at her.

"You sure you won't take that boat home? I'll manage somehow."

"Right, I take your engine room to pieces, and you think I'm going to leave it that way? I'm not leaving until this ship is ready to steam out of here, and I'll be running the engine room."

"No work tomorrow. Take the day off, have fun at the ball, I may drop in myself and claim a dance from you."

"I'll hold you to that." Cal grinned. "The next day we start the real work."

"Slave-driver." Captain Cully grinned back at Cal. "Get out of here."

Cal picked up her bundles from the cargo hold, added the uniform to the bundles then headed up to the hotel.

In the hotel room, she hid her uniform and one bundle beneath her bed, then rang for a bath. Once clean, she put on the dress Meireka had given her, picked up her satchel and headed down to the lounge.

Chapter 17 Fancy Dress

The lounge was crowded as usual, but Cal claimed the corner table and pulled out her sketchbook. It had been far too long since she had put pencil to paper.

Her fingers hadn't forgotten their skill. She put the patrons on paper. The older gentlemen drinking whisky and playing cards. A woman Cal guessed to be Crysabel's mother, looking around with a faint frown. The servers dancing between tables placing a drink there, a plate there. They all wore smiles, real ones, as Meireka had said.

Pentam and Crysabel came in and sat, leaning toward each other as they talked. Cal's pencil flew across the paper. Her art never lied. Cal looked at the finished drawing and wiped tears from her eyes. She should be happy for him. She *was* happy for him, but damn, it still hurt. Sir Shillingsworth walked into the lounge with the aid of a cane. Cal picked up the pencil again. Pentam waved him over and introduced him to Crysabel. Her father greeted them, and at their urging sat with them.

He looked unerringly across the room at Cal. She shook her head slightly. He lifted a shoulder a miniscule amount. Cal couldn't remember how they came to communicate so much with so little. She kept drawing, turning page after page. Capturing the angle of a face, the depth of a glance. Crysabel's hand reaching then pulling back.

Baroness Dimant saw her daughter and came over to haul her away, back to a table of people all the mother's age. Pentam looked bereft. Cal sketched his sorrow, how everything in his being yearned in one direction.

It was no longer toward Cal. She told herself it was a good thing. All part of her plan to save Pentam from himself. Cal put the sketchbook away. She picked up her satchel and sauntered over to Pentam.

"Hello, Pentam."

"Oh, hi." He turned away, then flushed red. "I'm a terrible person."

"Let's take some air on the terrace." Cal pulled him away from the table, catching a glimpse of Crysabel staring forlornly at them before turning back to her mother.

The terrace sat mostly in shade in the evening. Cal walked to the stone rail and leaned on it, so much like a ship's rail. Pentam stood beside her.

"Cal, I..." He stopped and looked down.

"Pentam." Cal took a deep breath and plunged in. "I love you, really. I always will. But I think you fell in love with me because I was the only woman on the ship you could protect. It wasn't really me, but your idea of who I was. This doesn't mean you don't love me, it means you need to love someone who wants adventure, and needs you to make them feel safe."

Cal handed him the sketchbook. Pentam took it, a frown on his face and flipped through, seeing the patrons, the servers. Stopping at the page which showed a man and a woman so clearly in love to anyone with eyes to see. He ran a finger across the page.

"You knew."

"Of course I knew," Cal said, then quieted her voice. "As soon as I met her, I saw she'd be perfect for you."

"And you told her to look me up, knowing I would..." Pentam's fists clenched.

"Not knowing, hoping. You deserve to be happy. You said it yourself, you were a coward around me. The whole trip, you worried about me, tried to protect me, keep me safe. I'll always treasure that. I'll always be your friend. Always. But I'll never be your wife." Cal turned away to look blurry-eyed at the harbour. "Get to know her, you already love her. Give her the adventure she craves, and keep her safe. I'd thought about traveling home with Father, making sure he made it safely, then returning with the parts for the Peregrine. I couldn't bring myself to watch you fall in love with someone else, as much as I need you to."

"But what about you?" Pentam sounded like he was choking. "You need love too."

"I'll find it someday. Someone who can love an Engineer First Class, who can stand to watch me do things which are mad, dangerous things, but nonetheless, need to be done. Until then, I have the Peregrine."

"You're leaving me for an *engine*?" Pentam's voice squeaked, then he started laughing until Cal joined him. They stopped, gasping for breath, face to face. He caressed her cheek. "Thank you, Cal. For everything. Be sure to visit whenever you're in the city." He walked away and didn't look back.

***

Cal walked into the hotel room to find Crysabel weeping on her bed.

"I should have known; he loves you so much."

"Crys, listen to me." Cal sat down on the bed and stroked the girl's back. "He does love me, and I love him, but I told you, that isn't enough. I informed him tonight I will never be his wife."

Crysabel sat bolt upright in bed and stared at Cal.

"You...set him free?" She threw her arms around Cal and held her. "Are you all right?"

Cal laughed and hugged Crysabel.

"I am. I know you'll make him deliriously happy. You are a kind, gentle soul. Exactly what he needs, and he will take you to see the world and be strong for you."

"And you stay with your ship?"

"For now." Cal let go of her friend. "I have something for you."

"You found a uniform?"

"Better."

Cal reached under the bed and pulled out the bundle with the gown and gloves and handed it to Crysabel.

The girl unwrapped it, then held it up.

"This is the dress you told me about."

"The dress which taught me I could be a lady and an engineer. I didn't have to choose."

"What do you think it will teach me?"

"You won't know until you wear to the ball."

Crysabel looked at the gown in wonder.

"Can I try it on?"

"Of course." Cal helped her friend out of her dress, then put the gown on her, gave her the gloves.

Crysabel looked in the mirror.

"It's like I'm in one of those fairy tales." She touched her reflection.

"You'll set the ball on fire, and no leaving at midnight." Cal pulled out a roll of paper and

219

flattened it on the table. "Sit and I'll draw your portrait."

"Now? But my eyes are all red."

"I won't draw your red eyes."

Crysabel sat in the chair with the grace Cal had seen in her from their first meeting. Her hair looked gold in the soft light. She looked young and vulnerable, but her eyes were determined.

As with Lord Carroway, Cal took her time, looking beneath the surface. Cal had a better idea of what she was doing and she put all her talent to work creating a portrait to speak for her.

When she'd finished, Cal treated the paper with the varnish, then called Crysabel over to look at it.

"Don't touch yet," Cal warned her, "not until tomorrow."

"That's me?" Crysabel was mesmerized by the portrait. "But I look strong, determined."

"Compassionate, gentle." Cal brushed her finger across Crysabel's cheek. "You are all those things and more."

Still in a daze, Crysabel took off the gown and hung it up carefully. She put the gloves on the dresser.

Cal tucked her into bed, then crawled into hers, strangely content after the events of the day.

***

Cal had thought the day would pass slowly, but it felt like she'd hardly got out of bed before the time had flashed by and they needed to dress for the ball.

They did each other's hair, or rather, Crysabel arranged Cal's hair and Cal called in Meireka to help with Crysabel's.

The two of them helped Crysabel into the gown, making sure it flowed exactly right. The gloves went on next. Cal put one of Crysabel's hats on her, then tied the feather necklace on.

"There, half the room will die of heart failure, the other half from jealousy." Cal adjusted the hat slightly and Meireka nodded.

Cal reach under the bed and pulled out her other bundle, she unrolled it and Crysabel laughed.

"You did get a uniform." She touched the gown. "You were right, this is better."

Meireka turned to leave when Cal started to change.

"Stay, we're all sisters here, and I have a favour to ask of you."

She pulled on the pants and set the crease just so, then the blouse; the jacket last with its gold insignia.

"You look amazing," Crysabel said. "This is going to be so much fun."

Cal handed Meireka a bundle of pencils and a few sketchbooks.

"Bring them over as soon as we're seated. Put them on a tray so it isn't obvious."

"You're going to draw all night?" Crysabel raised her eyebrows.

"Someone has to record the event." Cal grinned. She put her arm out. "Shall we go, Lady Crysabel?"

"We shall, Lady Cal."

Cal led down the stairs slowly, moving over to the big spiral stair for the last flight down to the ground floor. People stopped and turned to watch, then formed a path for them to walk through to the ballroom. It already churned with people, but they too stilled as the women entered. Pentam turned, then looked like he'd been struck by lightning. The music faltered briefly, then picked up again. Cal led Crysabel straight to him, and put her hand in his.

"Be good to each other." Cal bowed to them and backed away.

She turned to catch Baroness Dimant with an expression of wistfulness. It was quickly replaced with a frown as she headed toward her daughter. Cal intercepted her.

"Baroness Dimant." Cal took the woman's hand. "I'm Calliope Shillingsworth, Engineer First Class of the HMSV Peregrine." She guided the Baroness to a table where she had a good view of the room. Pentam and Crysabel were already dancing, soon joined by other guests.

"What is going on?" The Baroness leaned to look around Cal at the couple.

"Why did you bring Crysabel on a trip to see the world?"

"What? To show her the world, of course."

"One hotel looks much like another."

"Your point?" The Baroness glared at Cal.

"Pentam Booksdale is a scientist, soon to be a renowned scientist. He's the protégé of Sir Shillingsworth. Your daughter mentioned seeing his name at the museum. That will be Pentam's name soon. Then eventually he'll settle down as a professor to teach the next generation of explorers."

"Why should I care about some explorer?"

"Because your daughter cares. She wants to see the world, not hotels. Pentam can give her that, and he'll keep her safe."

"The girl is a romantic."

"Yes, she is, but also determined, kind and compassionate. The kind of person the world needs."

"She thinks I don't know about her orphans." The Baroness' lips twitched. "I fund that orphanage, there's nothing there I don't know about."

"So why let her sneak out?"

"If I just gave her permission, it would be too easy." The woman's face gave up the struggle and relaxed. Without her anger the Baroness was a handsome woman.

"She's going to change the world, Baroness, with or without you. Wouldn't it be so much more satisfying to be part of it?"

"And I suppose that young man...."

"He's going to help her. He is strong, loving, a gentleman. He'd lay down his life for her."

The Baroness sighed and dropped her head.

"I was young once." She lifted her head and squared her shoulders. "I'd better go be properly introduced."

Cal watched as the Baroness walked across the dance floor, couples sweeping out of her path. She reached Pentam and Crysabel. Pentam bowed over her hand. The Baroness touched Crysabel's cheek and said something which sent a bolt of joy across the girl's face and left Pentam looking dazed.

"I see it isn't just engines you fix." Captain Cully sat down beside Cal.

"Engines are easier, they don't break your heart."

"There now, don't be crying, it's unseemly for an Engineer First Class."

"I'm done crying."

"Well then, it's time for me to claim that dance." The Captain pulled her to her feet. The music and the workings of her mind sent her across the floor. For the moment, nothing else mattered.

***

The evening was winding down and Cal had filled the pile of sketchbooks. She carried them over to where Pentam and Crysabel sat hand in hand. The Baroness watching with a smile.

"Good evening." Cal bowed to them. "I have work to do tomorrow, so I will be off." She put the stack of sketchbooks on the table. "You may find these a good way to begin conversations." Cal turned and left the Baroness looking through the books.

In the hotel room, Cal rolled up Crysabel's portrait, then made sure everything else was packed and ready.

In the morning, the hotel buzzed with activity as the guests from the luxury ship got ready to return to the ship.

Cal found the team in the lounge.

"You sure about staying?" Dr. Franklyn looked at Lahdin and Dan.

"It will only be until the next ship. I will be back in time to help ready the presentation."

"Should be an interesting one for a change." Prof. Orthin chuckled. "This will make them sit up and take notice." He pointed at Pentam. "Going to make your reputation."

"I didn't do much."

"Don't be so modest. Those photographs along with Cal's drawings will change the way people record expeditions. Wouldn't be surprised if they don't put them in a book."

"Most of my journals will return with the samples. I will have something for Lord Carroway later." She put a pile of papers on the table. "I'll give these to you now, to show off on the voyage home."

"Safe travels, and I will see you in the city, sooner or later." Cal left before she could choke up. Sir Shillingsworth met her at the door.

"Remember I said I wasn't going to be an engineer?" Cal's mouth quirked. "I don't plan to just run the engines. I'm going to build them."

"I'd expect nothing less." Her father kissed her forehead. "I'm going to miss you."

"I will miss you too, Father. Take care of yourself and I'll see you when we get back to Anglia."

"I'll be at home, waiting for you. I'm going to pass the mantle to Pentam and work on writing my memoirs."

Cal hugged him, then went looking for Crysabel.

"I thought you'd be hard at work by now." Crysabel hugged Cal tight enough to drive the breath out of her. "Thank you, come and visit."

"I will."

"Young lady." The Baroness moved in front of Cal. "I believe I will take your advice." She looked over at Crysabel. "I hope you don't take too long to return, I can't imagine how much fun it would be to have an Engineer First Class as a maid of honour." The twinkle in the Baroness' eyes let Cal know where the girl got it from.

"I will make every attempt to be there."

Cal walked out of the hotel. Joliu waited beside her bag. She climbed into the cart and he set off for the Peregrine.

Chapter 18 The Royal Society

The bell from the bridge rang as the pointer on the dial moved to one quarter reverse. Cal checked the pressure yet again. Still holding steady at sixty. She rang back to the bridge in acknowledgement and turned the valve to send steam to the engine. Though she and Bran had spent an entire week running tests on the boiler, engine and the new shaft, Cal's heart went to her throat as the rumble of the engine grew. She still had trouble believing she'd made so many changes to the engine. In the end, she had to compromise her vision in the name of practicality.

There had been nothing wrong with the pistons. With a new shaft and shifting around of the various pipes and valves, the engine ran as good as new.

The vibration under her feet changed and the Peregrine moved freely in the water once again after six months in Finches Harbour.

Cal had enjoyed every minute of her stay, spending time with Meireka and Cericia. She'd left a stack of sketchbooks and pencils for the budding young artist. Meireka's husband took to guiding Lahdin and Dan through the jungle. Cal had joined them once. She preferred her ship.

The bell rang again. Cal moved the lever to shift to forward. It worked but her sketchbooks were full of ideas to make it even quicker and safer.

Once she put the engine in forward, she rang the bell. They'd stay at one quarter until they cleared the harbour.

"We'll get a bit of time before the next change." Cal looked over at her apprentice. His sailor's whites made his chocolate skin look even richer. "If you want to run up top to watch, go ahead, I'm fine here."

Joliu grinned and vanished. He'd been curious about the engine room, then intrigued enough Cal hired him to help with the heavy work. After that he'd become obsessed, so Cal had convinced Captain Cully to take the man on as apprentice engineer. Bran had his own trainee. The lad had tired of being cabin boy on the freighter which brought the new parts.

Hope everything arrived home in good shape.

Cal had supervised the transfer from the Peregrine to the Clyde, ensuring everything was secure. The Clyde's purser told her the ship could roll completely over and nothing would move. Her satchel held the only specimen she hadn't sent on the freighter. She hoped Pentam wasn't too put out by its absence.

She'd finished Lord Carroway's journal, copying drawings from her sketchbooks into a book she'd had made to order. On each facing page, she'd written a description for the image. Her heart would ache to give it away; it was probably the best work she'd ever done.

Maybe not; she thought of the portrait she'd done for Crysabel. Her friend had sent her a long letter telling Cal all about the voyage home. She and Pentam were engaged and they wanted to set the date for when Cal would be in the City. Cal had replied they were leaving port within the month and sent the letter with a ship heading home to Anglia.

The bells rang for half power, and Cal adjusted the valve then rang back. Joliu appeared a moment later.

"Thank you, Lady ma'am." He wiped his eyes.

"Just ma'am, when I'm on duty." Cal said and set him to polishing. She saw no reason why the engine room had to be dirty. They'd see how long the cleanliness lasted. The bridge signalled for full power and Cal let Joliu adjust the valve and respond to the bridge.

"That's it for now, we just watch the pressure, keep the water level up and shovel coal." Cal stretched and let the knot of tension run out of her shoulders. "Let's go over the workings of the engine room again."

***

Cal packed her kit, then straightened her dress whites and blue jacket. Bran would stay with the ship and keep working the trainees on maintenance needed between voyages. Captain Cully had given her a month of shore time while he sold his cargo and looked for another expedition to carry.

She couldn't delay any longer. Cal slung her bag over one shoulder, her satchel hanging beneath it and headed out on deck. She saluted Captain Cully before walking down the gangplank.

Hans waved at her from a new looking steam carriage. Cal ran over to hug him.

"Sir Shillingsworth wanted to come himself, but they are presenting to the Royal Society tonight. He needed to be there to help organize."

"Can we make it in time to listen?"

"Hold on tight." Hans put the carriage in gear and they sped off.

"How long before we need to top up the boiler?" Cal dropped her bag to the floor and watched as the world blurred past.

"Has an automatic feed, so theoretically we can make it to the city without stopping."

"The coal too?"

"As long as the pieces are small enough. A large chunk will gum up everything."

"I'm going to have to take a good look at it."

"After the talk."

"I have a month's shore leave. I could take the thing apart and put it back together in that time."

Hans laughed and swerved around a horse and cart.

***

Pentam let Crysabel adjust his suit yet again. The three scientists sat on the stage to the left of the podium. Sir Shillingsworth sat to the right.

"Almost time." Crysabel said. "You'll be fine."

Pentam peered through the curtains again.

"If she's there, you won't see her." Crysabel took Pentam's face in her hands. "She promised to try, and it would take a great deal to stop her. I'm looking forward to seeing her too." She kissed him on the lips.

"You have to be the least jealous person I've ever met."

"Cal's like a sister. How can I be jealous of my sister? Now if you start wandering after those society vixens who flock around you." Crysabel made a scratching motion with her hand held in a claw.

Pentam laughed.

"They terrify me more than the sea serpent."

"Did it really grow that big?"

"Yes, but we don't have any real evidence." Pentam sighed.

"But you said you found a tooth."

"And gave it to Cal." Pentam put his arms around his fiancée. "I can't be angry that she kept it, not after everything she's done for us."

"You're sweet." Crysabel adjusted Pentam's suit one last time. "Time to get started. I'll go around and sit with mother and father."

Pentam pushed through the curtain and walked out on stage. He'd watched Sir Shillingsworth do this many times; the man made it look easy. Pentam's knees shook. At the podium he took one last look through the audience, but with so many people he couldn't have spotted her if she was there.

Don't rush, you're in control. Sir Shillingsworth's voice rang in his head.

"Good evening, Lords and Ladies, men and women. Almost a year ago, Lord Carroway approached us to lead an expedition to the Sargasso Sea. I put together a team of top scientists in their field, along with their assistants, and under Sir Shillingsworth's capable direction hired the HMSV Peregrine to carry us to our destination. Before I go any further I'd like to thank Lord Carroway for his foresight in sponsoring this voyage." Pentam pointed to where Lord Carroway sat in his box. He waved and the crowd applauded politely. Pentam named the other sponsors, including his photography mentor Alistair McNaught who looked dazed to be included in the celebrated group.

"There is one member of the expedition not here tonight who I must acknowledge. Calliope Shillingsworth is the artist behind the drawings and sketchbooks you had a chance to look through before we started. You will have another chance at intermission and you are welcome to stay after the conclusion of our talk to explore them thoroughly. Interspersed among them are photographs I took with equipment loaned by Mr. McNaught. You will note that while the photographs show incredible detail, Miss Shillingsworth's work brings what she sees to life." Pentam took another long breath.

"We will begin our report with a brief summary of the chemistry of the Sargasso. I'll call on my partner Dan Komper to speak."

He waited for Dan, who'd refused to sit on stage, to climb up the steps and take the podium.

"Chemistry may seem boring, but everything around us is due to chemistry..."

The first half of the presentation went well, if quietly. The audience didn't get excited over chemical reactions or subtle differences in sea weed. Even the description of the fish they'd found only received spattered applause. While Dan, Dr. Franklyn and Prof. Orthin spoke, staff were uncovering specimen jars, bones, skins and other specimens.

234

During the intermission, the people looked through the displays, some pointing out details.

"It looks like I made the right choice to leave the expedition." Dr. Gostan planted himself in front of Pentam. "Nothing worth reporting. You should have just admitted you know nothing about chemistry and left the science to the real men."

"I'm so glad you came." Pentam forced a smile. He was saved from needing further response by Lord Carroway.

"It all looks marvelous. I can't wait to hear what you have for the second half. Have you seen Miss Shillingsworth?"

"Sadly, no." Pentam took the Lord's arm. "Have you had a chance to look at the portraits of the scientists and crew? If you'll come this way..." He walked past a furious Dr. Gostan.

Pentam looked out over the crowd. He didn't think they'd lost many people at intermission.

"I know you're waiting for the dramatic." Pentam waved at the stage. "I won't say exciting, because to a scientist, this is all exciting. I'll call on Lahdin to start off this portion of our presentation."

Lahdin came forward and talked about the life he'd discovered on the seaweed, starting with the tiniest creatures and working his way up. Once again staff were uncovering exhibits in the other hall, but Pentam and Lahdin had planned something to add the promised drama.

"...The sailors know how we scientists love to inspect everything closely and took to bringing things they'd found to us. Birds, for instance."

From the wings Dan opened the curtain enough to show a selection of seabirds, stuffed and mounted. Lahdin spoke about the species of birds, occasionally calling on one of the others for support.

"Not all the life we found needed to be looked at through a magnifying glass. Many larger crabs populated the seaweed." Dan pulled the curtain back a little further revealing a horde of crabs. "Prof Orthin will attest that they were not only fascinating to study, but delicious." The crowd laughed, finally getting animated and excited as more interesting things were revealed.

"The astonishing thing was the discovery of giant crabs whose legs spread over six feet across."

"Nonsense," Dr. Gostan's voice yelled from the crowd. "No crab can grow that big."

The curtain moved to reveal an immense crab mounted on a rough hatchway, threatening the crowd with its pincers. On the other side a preserving jar held another even larger specimen. The crew had brought them back along with the rudder from the derelict ship. Pentam had given them bonuses and thanked them profusely.

The gasps and muttering from the audience overwhelmed Dr. Gostan's objections.

"That isn't, however, the most astonishing find from our expedition." Lahdin waved Pentam up to the podium again. "I'll call on Pentam Booksdale to present this part of the evening."

"Fraud!" Dr. Gostan yelled. "He barely has an undergraduate degree."

"Sit down, you old coot. I want to hear this." Another voice boomed through the room and the audience muttered in support.

Pentam stepped up and took up giving the report as if there'd been no interruption. Sir Shillingsworth had said he was better to ignore the hecklers.

"While we were studying the activity of the birds over the seaweed Miss Shillingsworth noted an interesting pattern. All the species of bird we found were content to float on the ocean near the ship, none spent more than the briefest time on the seaweed. While watching our progress through a spyglass she saw something snatch a bird from the surface as easily as one of those birds would pick up a crab.

"The team devised a method by which we could capture and study whatever hunted the birds."

"Mr. Booksdale is being too modest." Prof. Orthin stood. "What he means is he came up with an elegant way to snare a potentially dangerous creature." The audience clapped as Pentam blushed.

"We set out in two boats..." Pentam described his plan, talking about how Cal had translated his idea from scribbles to a clear, concise process.

"After a long and boring afternoon," Pentam said, "nobody claims science doesn't have its dull moments, we were successful in capturing a creature never imagined to exist, though stories of them have been told by sailors for centuries." He drew out the moment as long as he dared.

"I present *serpens marinus calliope*." As the audience watched mouths agape, the curtains opened the rest of the way to show the largest of the serpents mounted. Women screamed and the gasps and muttering went on and on.

Once the room had quieted, Pentam described the chemistry and anatomy of the serpent.

"One last thing before you may return to look through the many displays and specimens set up for you in the main hall." Pentam and the team had long debates on whether to talk about the large serpent. Pentam insisted they had no evidence, the others argued that as scientists, their observations were evidence. The rest of the team won the argument.

"We'd captured three of the *serpens marinus calliope* but were determined to bring more specimens home for study. The process had become routine, and we got careless. A large creature snagged our net, almost swamping our boats. The rope tangled around my leg and dragged me out of the boat and under the water. Tragically, one of our crew had lost his life in this same way, but we hadn't put the pieces together. The only reason I stand before you today is the immediate and brave action by Miss Shillingsworth who dove in after me with a knife in her teeth and pulled herself down to me. I have never been so happy to see a woman with a knife. After cutting myself free, we were helped to the surface by a member of the Peregrine's crew, Thomas Bondry.

"You will understand that after this close call, Captain Cully and Sir Shillingsworth decided it was time to return home. Yet fate intervened. While fishing off the stern of the Peregrine, catching one last supper of fresh fish, I attracted the attention of the large serpent. Once again I owe my life to Miss Shillingsworth, who spotted the danger and warned me in time to escape the creature. The ship wasn't so fortunate, losing its rudder and taking damage in the engine room."

"Stuff and nonsense." Dr. Gostan stood up and pointed at Pentam, red in the face. "I suppose you have a giant sea serpent hidden in your pocket."

"Dr. Gostan has apparently granted himself a doctorate in biology as well as chemistry." Pentam had to grip the podium hard to stop himself from collapsing at the sound of that voice. His heart leaped in happiness.

"You understand why my father removed him from the expedition's roster. We had no desire to spend months at sea with such a boorish man."

Dr. Gostan's mouth was moving but Pentam couldn't hear him over the noise of the audience as they turned to find the source of the new interruption.

Cal strolled down the aisle of the auditorium, dressed in immaculate whites with a blue jacket. Her hair had been cut short, yet still somehow looked feminine.

"May I introduce Miss Calliope Shillingsworth, artist extraordinaire and engineer of the Peregrine." Pentam pointed toward Cal. The room erupted in applause, completely drowning out Dr. Gostan who finally slumped down in his seat looking petulant.

Cal made her way up the stairs to the podium.

"Sorry I was late, we ran into a spot of trouble with the steam carriage. It took me longer than it should have to set it right." She hugged Pentam. "I caught enough to know you are doing a marvelous job."

Cal turned to the podium and stood straight at attention, yet somehow projecting her complete control over the situation.

"As my dear friend Pentam was explaining, the serpent damaged the rudder and the engine room. The chief engineer, Monky, was blinded in the incident. I expect he is here tonight as he returned to Anglia with my father and the rest of the team.

"As you can imagine, being without an engine or means to steer the ship was a concern..."

Pentam stood back and marvelled at how Cal immediately captured the imagination of the audience. She told the story of setting her assistant engineer to work on the damage to the boiler, while she built a steam cannon to go after the monster. There was no hint of boasting in the matter of fact account of the construction, set up and use of the steam cannon.

"As you may guess, we weren't in a position to recover the body of the large serpent. Yet it did leave something behind for us. Something which Mr. Booksdale discovered and gave to me, and now, I return it to him to complete the display from our expedition."

Cal pulled the tooth from her satchel, and even this competent, strong Cal needed two hands to lift it to where the audience could see.

Screams and shouts came from all sides of the auditorium, then the applause started as Cal passed the tooth to Pentam.

They waited until the pandemonium had quieted enough to speak.

"The members of the team will be available in the display hall to answer questions. Refreshments will be served." Pentam waved at the team to stand beside him, insisting on bringing the assistants up too. They were mobbed as soon as they entered the display hall.

***

"My heavens, I've never seen such a show." Lord Carroway poured drinks for Pentam, Sir Shillingsworth and Cal. The rest of the team had headed in their separate directions, already booked to speak across the country.

"I must admit to a certain satisfaction in putting Dr. Gostan in his place." Cal swirled her brandy. "But most of it was down to Pentam."

"He was very good." Lord Carroway agreed. "I've been to plays with less drama and excitement."

"I have something for you." Cal drew the journal out of her satchel. "This could be some of the best work I've ever done." She handed it to him.

Lord Carroway opened it and began to go through the pages, his expression changing with each picture. He closed it, and sighed.

"I will look at it later, when it wouldn't be rude of me to give it the concentration it deserves. It will be a center piece of my collection. I've decided to open it to the public once a week for now, I'll see how it goes."

"Speaking of your collection." Pentam sat back with a satisfied look. "There will be some deliveries over the next few days. I know you sent the preserving jars, but we have a number of mounted specimens for you. I think they will show better if you're opening to the public."

Lord Carroway's eyes lit up. "One of those crabs? I'd love one of the crabs."

"We certainly have a crab for you. The crew brought us a nice selection. But I'm sure it will be overshadowed by your sea serpent."

Cal worried Lord Carroway would drop dead from shock.

"A sea serpent? But you said you only caught three."

"That's right." Cal leaned forward. "One for the Royal Museum, one for the University to study, and one for the man with the vision to sponsor the expedition. Not even the curator at the museum argued the point. With you letting people visit, we'll start a whole new wave of interest in science and exploration."

Chapter 19 And Then ...

Cal wandered into the dining room and saw her father with his tea and a mountain of books stacked around him.

"How are the plans for the memoirs?"

"If I try to write about everything I've done, the book would fill a library. Whittling down the pile is turning out to be more of a chore than I'd thought."

"Pick the stories that changed your life."

"No one wants to read about when I met your mother, or the day you were born."

Cal poured herself tea and put jam on a slice of bread.

"I don't know, it wouldn't be a bad thing to have a human side to the fearless explorer, remind people you cared about more than discovering the world."

"Do you mind if I use some of your sketches from over the years?"

"Mind? Of course not, I did them for you."

"I guess we'd better finish up and get dressed, the Baroness will not be pleased if we are a second late."

"Not every day you get to marry off your only daughter." Cal stood up and saw the look of pain cross Sir Shillingsworth's face. "It's OK, Father, I don't plan on staying single my whole life. I'm waiting to find someone who doesn't throw a fit if I have to fix an engine or slay a monster."

"Don't wait too long."

Cal laughed and hugged her father.

"I'm in no rush."

Hans deposited them outside the church, then drove home with the steam carriage. The crusher she'd added, powered from the main engine, kept the coal from jamming up, but Hans didn't quite trust it yet.

"Come, come, Sir Shillingsworth, the Baron is waiting for you. Tell him some of your wonderful stories so he doesn't wear his shoes out pacing the floor. Calliope, dear, come with me." The Baroness walked into the cathedral and through a side door. "Your Captain Cully has come with a few of the crew. Could you greet them and make them comfortable?" She opened the door and let Cal in. "I'll be back in a few minutes to take you to Crysabel."

"Hello, Cal." Henrichs waved. "Tragic news. The Captain has kicked me off his ship. Seems he needed a Captain for another tub, now that every peer in the land wants to send expeditions out across the seven seas."

"Congratulations, I guess." Cal saluted.

"The boat's a disaster. Engine room is outdated, hull needs fixing. Doesn't even have a decent crane."

"I see." Cal looked over to see a wicked grin on Captain Cully's face.

"I want Joliu, and I'll need another trainee."

"Two." Henrichs' mouth twitched.

"What are you plotting?" Cal looked at Henrichs severely, then back at Captain Cully.

"We were talking." Captain Cully came over. "About what a terrible waste it is to leave you locked up in the engine room."

"I *like* the engine room." Cal's heart thumped.

"I need a first mate." Henrichs grabbed Cal's numb hand and shook it.

"First mate?"

"You have a gift for command." Captain Cully put his arm around her shoulders. "I want you to develop it. No reason you shouldn't have your own ship someday, maybe not too far away."

"I need a first-class engineer, but once you have the engine room running, anyone can run it." Henrichs put her arm on around Cal's shoulder from the other side. "How about it?"

"How can I win against you two?" Cal grinned. "It will be an honour to serve with you."

"Welcome to the Kestrel." Henrichs pumped Cal's hand again.

The others in the room, Thomas, Bran, and Joliu, cheered.

The Baroness opened the door as if she'd been signalled.

"That jacket you have is very nice, but a bit plain." She lifted a jacket up and handed it to Cal. "Try it on, we used Crysabel as a model."

"First mate's braid? How long have you been plotting this?"

"Henrichs wanted to make you second mate on the Peregrine, but once we needed the new ship, this works even better." Captain Cully took her old jacket and nodded his head as Cal tried on the new one. "Looks good on you." He took her engineer's pin and transferred it to the new one.

"Come on, Crysabel has been bursting keeping this a secret." The Baroness tugged at Cal's arm.

Cal followed her to the room where Crysabel wore a gown which blended the best of the city's high fashion and the gown from Finches Harbour.

"You look beautiful." Cal carefully hugged her friend. "I couldn't be happier for you and Pentam."

"What do you think of your promotion?" Crysabel grinned at her. "I just about died when they told me, and I couldn't say anything. The jacket looks good on you. I can't wait to sail with you."

"Sail with me?" Cal shook her head; things were happening too fast for her to keep up.

"I insisted our first voyage be on your ship. Pentam's talking about visiting some islands on the other side of the world."

"And when does he plan to leave?"

"He's found some people already to come, maybe in a couple of months? Pentam said if anyone could get the Kestrel in shape it would be you."

"Wonderful."

"Almost time." The Baroness clapped her hands and the bridesmaids lined up, each holding a small bouquet.

A boy in a suit opened the door and they began the entry into the cathedral. Soon it was Cal's turn. She breathed deeply, straightened her back and walked down the aisle. There was a collective gasp from the congregation, then from somewhere near the front clapping began until it rang through the church.

Pentam smiled and nodded to her. Cal broke with the plan and shook his hand.

Then Crysabel entered the sanctuary and an astonished look washed over him. Cal watched the bride enter on the Baron's arm. She looked every bit as besotted as Pentam.

**

After the wedding, a select group were invited to tea in the Royal Gardens. Cal wandered about taking in the celebration. Crysabel and Pentam stood hand in hand greeting people.

"You would be First Mate and Engineer of the HMSV Kestrel?"

Cal turned to look at a man about her father's age. He looked familiar, maybe a relative of the Baron?

"That would be me." Cal inclined her head.

The man smiled broadly.

"You put on quite a show at the Royal Society."

"Mostly Pentam's doing."

"An extraordinary young man. I will be keeping an eye on him, maybe get involved in one of his expeditions." He offered Cal his arm and they walked through the gardens.

"I'm sure he would be delighted to have you along."

"Now that *would* be a treat, but sadly mother doesn't like me leaving the country for long periods of time." The gentleman reached down and removed a dead flower from its stem.

"A pity."

"Nonetheless, I get to enjoy the excitement vicariously through the Royal Society for Science."

"It's a wonderful idea, to have the Society. It keeps the people interested in the sciences and exploration."

"I'm glad you approve." The man smiled as if he had a huge secret.

Cal's heart raced. She was missing something, something immensely important. Her hand trembled as they turned to head back to the party. The Baroness looked in their direction, then her jaw dropped. *God, who is this guy?*

"The Royal Society for Science, wasn't it started—"

"By the Crown Prince of Anglia. Yes."

Cal closed her eyes. It hit like a bolt of lightning.

"What am I supposed to do, your Highness?"

"Walk and enjoy our conversation, Calliope." The Crown Prince put his hand on hers. "It's a delight to be able to talk with someone without worrying about the protocol. It is as tiresome for me as for the people I meet."

"Since you are here, your Highness, would you care to greet the happy couple?" Cal led him over to where Crysabel and Pentam stood, taking a break from greeting people to stare into each other's eyes.

"Pentam, Crysabel," Cal spoke firmly to get their attention. "May I present, his Royal Highness, the Crown Prince Hubert." She stopped at a gentle squeeze from the Crown Prince's hand on her arm.

Crysabel curtseyed gracefully as she did everything, while Pentam bowed low.

"We are honoured, your Highness."

"I am pleased to be here on such a happy day." The Crown Prince lifted Crysabel and Pentam, then kept hold of their hands. "My mother sends her greetings. She approves of my interest in the sciences."

Cal had stepped back wishing fiercely that she had her sketchbook and a pencil. She felt something pushed into her hand.

"Please?" the Baroness whispered.

Cal took the tiny diary and sketched the scene as fast as she could and still capture the likeness on the small page.

The Prince looked over at Cal.

"Let's see it."

Cal handed him the book. He examined it carefully.

"I'm impressed, you're very quick and I truly look like I should." He put his hand out. "Pencil."

Cal handed it to him and he signed the opposing page.

Congratulations. HRH Hubert.

"Here, a keepsake for your special day." He handed the book to Crysabel, who held it as if it were made of gold. He turned to Pentam. "Fine presentation the other night, thoroughly enjoyed it. Send to my office when you're planning your next expedition. I would be delighted to contribute." The Prince nodded at them, then sauntered away.

***

Cal checked her bag and her satchel. She had everything.

"Back to work, Father." She gave him a hug.

"Be safe, write me about your travels."

Cal left the house, refusing to turn back. She expected to see Hans waiting with the steam carriage, instead a gilded coach waited on the road. A young man jogged over to Cal.

"First Mate and Engineer of the HMSV Kestrel?"

Cal nodded.

"The Crown Prince's compliments, he would like to speak with you on a matter of importance."

"Let's not keep him waiting then." The young man looked a bit shocked but recovered quickly and led her to the Coach. He opened the door to reveal the Crown Prince seated inside.

Cal bowed. "Your Highness."

"Come, Calliope, we walked together in the gardens." He waved her into the coach. The young man closed the door and they headed off down the road.

"Your Highness, a Prince may presume to break protocol. A First Mate may not."

He sighed.

"You are right of course. You remind me of my daughter. In a way, she is the reason I have abducted you." He sat back and sized her up. "Tell me more about this steam cannon you built."

"The cannon was an act of desperation, your Highness. We needed to get the rudder, and the sea serpent swam between us and it. I had the engine room in as good a shape as possible, but without a rudder, it was useless."

"You used an oak shaft for the weapon? How effective was it?"

"Your Highness, it blew a hole right through the sea serpent killing it instantly. It sounds like a powerful weapon, but we were lucky. The tank had started to deform, another few minutes it would have blown and taken us, and probably the ship to the bottom of the ocean."

"What if you wanted to move something slowly?"

"You'd be better off running a steam engine and setting the gears to whatever speed you want. Steam is highly compressible, water is not, which is why it's important to keep the water level right, too high and you have little volume to work, too low and the pressure won't hold."

"Fascinating. So you could use water to lift or lower heavy objects?"

"There is no reason why not. Don't you have engineers working for you?" Cal lowered her head. "My apologies, I shouldn't be presumptuous."

The prince laughed.

"In private you may be as presumptuous as you need. In answer, yes, we have engineers, but they are old, hidebound, already thinking in terms of tradition and what's already been done. I need people who don't know what's impossible, like someone who builds a steam cannon to kill a monster."

"I am at your service, your Highness."

"Calliope, you are a delight."

"Your Highness, I'm going to be presumptuous again and ask you to call me Cal. Calliope always makes me wince."

"Cal." The Prince paused as if tasting the name. "It suits you."

The coach slowed and stopped. The Prince jumped out and held his hand out to Cal. She had no choice but to let him help her from the coach.

"My daughter married a prince in Ferandica. Not the Crown Prince, but second or third in line. She wrote to me that the Crown Prince would be visiting and to expect him soon. It normally takes a week of travel for someone to journey between our countries. He arrived in three days in that." The Prince pointed up. A huge ship floated high above the field.

"I've heard about airships." Cal stared up in awe. "But I've never seen one, and I didn't imagine it would be so big."

"He brought twenty people with him, and has been insufferably smug about it. Good thing we're on friendly terms."

"So you want the lift to raise and lower people and cargo to the airship?"

"I knew you were the right choice. The others stared at me and told me it had never been done."

"I will research and experiment." She looked wistfully at the airship. "I have an obligation to the Kestrel."

"I need you on the Kestrel, Cal, learning how to command, what it takes to run a ship. Learn it from top to bottom. Then come back and build me one of those." He pointed up.

"Are you crazy?" Cal peered up at the ship. "It floats, so somehow it is lighter than the air. How? They journeyed here in three days, so they have an engine, and I see two propellers. How did they build it light enough? How much coal do they need, how much water? Every ounce they put on board means that much more lift, somehow. It doesn't even begin to address what it's made of—"

"The fact you're asking those questions makes you the right person to do it. You won't be alone. I have others working on it. They'll send you ideas by Royal packet. If we know your itinerary, it will be simple."

Cal stared at him.

"You really expect me to do this."

"What if an unfriendly country builds one? They could float over us dropping bricks on our heads."

"Bricks would be too heavy. Their ship wouldn't be able to take off."

"Fine, feather pillows." The Prince flipped his hand in irritation. "We need to have our own ships, and we need to use them for peaceful purposes."

"Because they'll assume we have a fleet in reserve." Cal straightened up and faced him to salute. "Your Highness, I will do this, somehow."

"That's what I wanted to hear. Now, we'll do this again later with all the fancy dress and foofaraw, next time you're on shore." The prince pulled something from his pocket. He handed her a tiny scroll. "Stand still and let me pin this on."

Cal looked down to see a gold gear, hanging from a star with the crown engraved on its center.

"What?"

"You are the very first of my Royal Engineers, Lady Calliope Shillingsworth. The scroll is a Royal Warrant allowing you to commandeer aid from any embassy or ship under our flag.

There's some boring stuff about budgets and such, you'll get a letter."

Cal ran her finger across the star. "Lady?"

"I can't have stuffy peers giving you a hard time, it will interfere with your work."

"Can you please call me Cal?"

The Crown Prince laughed. "Cal, I promise, when there's no need to be formal." He took her elbow and guided her back to the coach. "Time to get to work, Royal Engineer."

He helped her in, then climbed in after her and rapped on the ceiling.

Cal knew it was impossibly rude, but she couldn't help herself. She gazed, entranced, out the window of the coach at the airship until it finally dropped out of sight.

Acknowledgements

This book took a winding path to creation. An author friend asked me about doing a collection of sea serpent stories, which started the gears turning. Another friend was putting together an anthology with the theme of twilight. Not quite one thing or another, which brought in the Sargasso Sea. In the end neither of those projects worked out, but I loved the story, and especially Calliope so much I turned the short story into a novel.

Like every book, this one was a team effort. Heidi Lyn Burke beta read the original short story and her comments were invaluable for the novel.

Then Lorend Boyes, Deborah Dunson, Pierre Lemoine, Susan Fritz and Alex Quinlan beta read the novel version. My good friend and editor Dean C. Moore copy edited the book, and Krista Burdine did the proofreading.

Abigail Horne, a talented young artist created the interior sketches for me, and the cover is designed by A.P. Fuchs.

About the Author

Alex is an author, editor and reviewer living in Winnipeg, Manitoba overlooking the Assiniboine River. He has two dogs who drag him out for walks, and a scotch collection to celebrate the successful completion of his next goal.

Alex McGilvery

About the Illustrator

Abigail Horne is a talented artist. I saw her work first on the cover of one of her father's books. I immediately knew I wanted her to do the interior illustrations.

As a child, Abigail Horne fell in love with art. She is currently in the Studio Art and Plan II Honors Programs at the University of Texas in Austin. Her hope is to become a counselor and Art Therapist. For now, she is happy teaching her passions and skills to younger students.

Learn more at artbyabigail.com

Other books by Alex

Wendigo Whispers
The Devil Reversed
Generation Gap
The Gods Above
Tales of Light and Dark
Like Mushrooms (poetry and photography)
The Heronmaster
Blood and Sparkles, and other stories
Princess of Boring
By the Book
Sarcasm is My Superpower
Playing on Yggdrasil
The Unenchanted Princess

Alex also has stories in:

Words on the Rocks
Beyond the Wail
Collidor Stream Collection 2016

Read short stories and excerpts from his novels at alexmcgilvery.com